Addicted To Heartache:

From one man's bed to the next

A novel

By: Tamyra Walker

Acknowledgements

First, I give honor to God, who is the head of my life. He is the reason I am breathing this very moment. It is because of him that I have the activities of my limbs, and also that I have completed my third book. It is truly an honor to share this work with you. It has been a long time coming, and I thank God for trusting me with this precious gift of writing. As long as I live, I will always bring you the very best that I can. You all deserve nothing less than my very best.

To my models: Tiffany Brown, Markese Grant, Robert Charles Means, Tommy Perryman, and Tamara Walker, I thank each one of you for agreeing to grace the front cover of my book. All of you did an exceptional job. I have no doubt in mind that you were the best choices I could have made for the cover. I wish you well in every endeavor and I truly hope that you enjoy the book. Lowndes County represented for this project. I can truthfully say that the world is not ready for you ladies and gentlemen. Stay tuned for part two... that's for whoever survived part one.

I thank all of my supporters and readers. Of course I write for myself first, but it is an honor to have so many people who trust my writing and who patiently wait for anything I write to be released. I give a special shout out to Tracey Thomas, Wanda Steele, and Cynthia Jackson (also from Lowndes County 4/5). You ladies truly rock. You definitely know how to make a girl feel good. Thank you so much for believing in me and not being afraid or reluctant to support me.

To a dear friend of mine, Quentin Brown. Almost 25 years ago, you vanished out of my life without a trace. We were both teens. We shared a bond that many wouldn't understand. I searched aimlessly for you for a long time. But to no avail. I didn't think our paths would ever cross again. But obviously, God had a different plan. I thank you for your unwavering support. It is so much more than I could have ever asked for. I wish you well in whatever you do in life. I'm sure you know already that you can achieve whatever it is that you put your mind to. I dedicate this book to you. Thank you for being a great friend.

Prologue

"Get the crash cart. She's coding." Jamie Ferrell, ran as fast as her feet would carry her to ICU room number nine in the SICU department at Mercy Memorial Hospital. She was the unit manager and had been manning the nurses' station when she noticed a patient's heart rate running in the mid-thirty's.

Every nurse in the unit was already crowded around the fifty-five-year old school teacher who had been shot by a terrorist at St. Peter's Elementary school… the school she'd been a faithful teacher at for over 20 years. All ten of the other victims had already succumbed to their injuries, three girls, four boys, a maintenance guy, and two other school teachers. And, now it looked as if Mrs. Santiago, the fourth grade math teacher who was shot while using her body as a human shield to keep two of her students from getting shot, wasn't going to make it either.

"Roll her over. Let's get the backboard under her." Jamie stepped up on the stool next to the bed and placed the heel of her hands in the middle of Mrs. Santiago's chest. She clasped them together. "One, two, three, four, five," She said, counting compressions. A surge of adrenaline ran through her body like electricity. "Six, seven, eight, nine, ten."

Tamyra Walker

This poor lady was at work, educating our youth when that piece of shit aimed his gun at her head, she angrily thought, trying unsuccessfully not to allow her emotions to take control of her ability to run the code.

"Eleven, twelve, thirteen, fourteen, fifteen." Jamie continued counting compressions, while the assistant Unit Manager, LaCheryl Longmire, ventilated the patient with the Ambu bag.

"Stay with us, sweet lady. This world need more people like you." Jamie said through clenched teeth. She straddled Mrs. Santiago and continued compressing her heart. It was a harrowing and surreal experience. But Jamie was determined and that was what made her such a great nurse- her willingness to go to bat for all of her patients, even when there seemed to be no flicker of hope.

Another nurse took over the compressions while Jamie pushed the Vasopressin, Atropine, and other medicines through the IV.

I'll bet your husband... children... friends all love you, so much. You seem like such a nice person. I probably would have loved for you to be my teacher. Jamie's thoughts were on a rampage as she continued her quest to revive Mrs. Santiago, who had been teacher of the year in her district for three consecutive years. *I know your hubby can't wait for you to return home to him so the two of you can continue watching "Wheel of Fortune together." I'm going to get you back to him. I promise, sweet lady. I'm not going to let him down.*

Jamie glanced at the nurse now doing the compressions. She could clearly see that she was exhausted.

"Move," She said, lightly shoving her to the side. "I'll do it. One... two... three... four... five... Come on Mrs. Santiago, come on, sweetie. You got to pull through. You just have too."

To no avail, Mrs. Santiago's heart rhythm still went into Asystole.

"Time of death, 3:05 p.m.," the hospitalist said after twenty-five minutes. He looked at Jamie with compassion. He knew that she had a hard time accepting that patients sometimes die. He knew that this death was going to take its toll on her.

A look of desperation covered Jamie's face. "We didn't try hard enough... we can still save her," She said as she began to count compressions again. Her uniform top was now covered in blood. Her hair was matted to her head from the perfusion of sweat. But Jamie didn't care. All she could think about was Mrs. Santiago... an educator, who had no idea that when she left home that morning to go to work she would never return.

A set of hands gently touched her on the shoulder. "We did all we could do, Ferrell. She's gone." Jamie looked at Mrs. Santiago lying atop the bed and her heart sunk to her toes. She had dark black hair that only had a few strands of gray. Her face was just about as smooth as a baby's bottom. She had a tiny mole above her lip. A look of peace was the only make-up she wore.

The respiratory therapist walked past Jamie, pushing the ventilator he had just disconnected. The only thing left was the tube sticking out of Mrs. Santiago's mouth. Jamie shook her head, pulled off her gloves, stormed out of the ICU room and rushed to the bathroom, tears gushing down her face. She leaned her head over the toilet and vomited for what seemed like forever.

"It's so unfair." She said inaudibly. "It's so motherfucking unfair." She stood there, trembling from the hurt and anger she felt. Her heart was beating so fast that she thought she would faint for sure.

"Oh, why, God? Please, tell me why." Jamie held onto the sink, balling her eyes out until she heard one of her nurses knocking on the door.

"Are you alright in there, Jamie?" LaCheryl yelled through the door.

Jamie looked at her reflection in the mirror over the sink. Her eyes were red and swollen, her hair in disarray. She turned on the faucet, splashing cold water on her face.

"I'll be out in a sec."

She dried the lingering tears from her face, took a deep breath and unlocked the door.

LaCheryl stood face to face with Jamie. She leaned over and hugged her tightly. Jamie allowed her body to relax in her arms.

"I wanted her to make it." She said, another tear escaping down her face.

"I know you did, boss." LaCheryl gently massaged her shoulders. "We all did!"

Jamie expelled an aggravated breath from her lungs. "So what's going on now?"

"Nothing. You have a phone call, boss."

Jamie nodded her head but didn't say anything. She released herself from LaCheryl's tight grip and walked to her office feeling defeated. "This is Jamie." She said, picking up the call on line two."

"Hello, sweetheart. Are you ready for our date tonight?"

As bummed as she felt, Jamie couldn't help feeling a smile come across her face. "I'm as ready as I'll ever be, baby. I can't wait to see what you have planned." Jamie disconnected the call. She took one last deep breath as she picked up her workbag, grabbed her car keys and walked out the door. "Rest in peace, Mrs. Santiago," she mumbled as she made her way to the parking deck.

Chapter 1

'There isn't a man alive that will have me so stupefied that I will sit brooding over him. I'm no shrinking violet, and if he doesn't want me, well, that's too bad. There's more fish in the sea. I just hope I don't have to kiss a lot of frogs before I find my Prince Charming'

~ Jamie Ferrell ~

~*~

"Girl, he made a fool out of her!" Marlena's drunken voice echoed throughout the women's bathroom. She and her best friend, Donna, entered the lady's room, their high heel's clacking against the tiled floor, staggering, as they grabbed hold of the marble counter top to hold themselves steady.

A couple of martini's, a tequila, a Long Island Iced tea, and a couple of Budweiser's later, and they were sloppy drunk… barely able to walk without falling all over themselves. They wore cheap, off the clearance rack, simply fashion dresses that hardly left anything to the imagination. You could see everything that God had blessed them with in plain view. That included the shape of their vaginas and the cellulite on Donna's thighs. Donna also had a quarter-sized scar from being

7

stabbed on her back. It peeked from under the back of her bra as if it were playing peek-a-boo.

Marlena was a size zero. Her one-shoulder, tight, hot pink, see through around the breast dress didn't look as sleazy as Donna's strapless, gold, costume looking dress that just came past her butt cheeks. She had so many tracks glued in her head that her neck should have snapped back from the weight of it all. But you couldn't tell her that she wasn't cute. Let her tell it, she was the next top model that the world wasn't ready for.

The singer, Joe, was the guest of honor at a birthday bash that one of their conquests, Ayanna Fason, from the same projects Marlena grew up, had thrown for her thirty-second birthday. Donna and Marlena all but threw their panties on the stage at him while he sang, *All of the Things Your Man Won't Do*, flipping the bird finger to anyone who gave them the side-eye.

Surprisingly, when Donna first got the invite she didn't appear to be too thrilled to attend the party. She rolled her eyes as she read the calligraphic penmanship, written in blue ink on a piece of card stock. She sucked her teeth and looked at Marlena. Jealousy swam in her eyes like it was a lifeguard.

"Dang, that bitch always trying to outshine everybody else. Done used her whole damn income tax trying to act like she balling. Her ole

Section-8 having ass! She knows she need to be buying some decent clothes for them snotty nose children that she loves to leave on everybody. Probably don't know who they daddies is anyway." She threw the invitation in her purse, and grabbed her compact to make sure her fake, thicker than cottage cheese eyelashes weren't falling off. She was still reeling from the embarrassment that she'd felt when one of the last pair she had fell off into her Terriyaki at Shogun a couple of months back. She felt she would surely die if such a mishap occurred again.

When she knew that she was straight, she made her way over to the drink machine to buy herself a Coke.

"Maybe so." Marlena chimed in. She blew a bubble, popping her gum back to back. "But my ass is going to be there… front and center, boo. I might find me a man, ya know." She popped her gum again and glanced at Donna. "Are you coming or are you going to throw shade all day?"

Donna rolled her eyes at Marlena and stuck her middle finger up.

"You know what to do with this, don't you? It's not shade when you are speaking facts. Remember that, boo."

"Whatever," Marlena said. "I asked you a question. Are you going to be there or not?"

Tamyra Walker

"And you know it, girl." Donna popped the top on her coke and took a long swig. "Shiiiiiid, I might find me a nice side-piece. Somebody to pick up Marcus's slack. With his tired ass." Suddenly her voice was filled with a hint of aggravation.

Marlena shook her head like she couldn't believe that Donna was still even dealing with Marcus's no- good behind. But she didn't reply. That was a battle she did not feel like fighting. Donna had been like silly putty in Marcus's hand ever since they first met some three and a half years ago when Donna was getting her GED, and Marcus was enrolling in school to get his. He was hardly anybody to get excited about with his lanky body, semi-bird lips, and beady eyes, spread evenly over blue-black skin. He wore his hair in an unkempt fade that didn't fit the sculpture of his face. He was a far cry from good looking. That only meant one thing. He was packing elsewhere, and that kept Donna slithering back into his web, time and time again.

Marcus was your typical, scam anybody he could type of guy. He would've never dreamt of sitting still for any amount of time in a classroom setting, but there was nothing that he loved more than money. He wanted a job at the Mercedes plant so he could continue his lifelong dream of having all of the unnecessary things that wouldn't have enhance his life the least. It was very important to him to appear to others to be something that he was not. He realized that having a job at the Mercedes plant would only be a pipe dream if he *didn't have a high school diploma. He still didn't get the job because he failed to pass the pre-employment drug test. That was the first night that he hit Donna, and he has been hitting her ever since. He could black her eye and she would still lay with him the same night and give him her money, too. She honestly didn't have a right to talk about Ayanna. At least Ayanna had sense enough to splurge on herself and not a man who only wanted what he felt like she could offer him. The year before, Donna had given Marcus half of her income tax to put rims on his car. He then beat her when she wouldn't give him another $500 to put a new stereo system in it. He came to her with one of his bullshit apologies a couple days later and of course she had forgiven him. After banging her for a couple of hours, she rolled over on her side and reached in her wallet to give him the five-hundred dollars.*

"Thanks, boo." He said smiling, flashing a gold-plated grill that was the same color as the wrapper on those little bunnies you could get from Family Dollar around Easter time. "You know I appreciate this. Thanks for holding a brother down."

Marlena and Donna both laughed loudly, twerking their butts. They couldn't wait to see if either one of them could possibly slip Joe their number, maybe even have him for the night too, in his hotel suite. They were even willing to engage in a menage a trois if it came to that. As long as he put a little something in their pocket at the ending

11

of the night, he could have his way with them. He could have an encore, too.

"How about you be my man, boo?" Donna's voice slurred as she yelled out into the crowd. I want more, and more, and after that- more and more." Marlena twisted her lips and looked at Donna.

"Ugh, you need to get it together, honey." She whispered. She could hold her alcohol a little better than Donna. The only way anyone could tell she was drunk was if someone made her mad. When she was drunk and mad, you literally had hell on your hands and had to peel her off the person who rubbed her the wrong way.

"Come with me. Let's go to the little girl's room." Marlena demanded.

"But I want more, and more." Donna objected, while her friend practically pulled her in the direction of the bathroom.

"Get your drunk ass in here and pull yourself together, bitch." Marlena snapped.

"Dang bestie... calm down." Donna pretended like she was pouting.

She pulled her mac eyeliner out of her knock-off Michael Kors purse and threw it on the counter. It took her applying a couple extra layers of make-up to compete with Marlena's beautiful face, that was usually only covered with just a hint of lip gloss on her full lips. But Donna was endowed, in the hips and butt department. She had one of those bodacious butts that made any dress she wore rise a couple of inches. That wasn't all. She also had a nice set of breasts that loved to spill out her tight-fitting blouses and lowcut dresses that she wore daily. Even when Donna went to church, she had to look sexy. She was always on the hunt for her next sugar daddy. It was very important to her that she was taken care of without having to break a sweat or nail in the process. Most times, she would come up with the short end of the stick. However, she never gave up hope. She was a persistent little hood rat. Donna looked at Marlena and smirked.

"Are you talking about Vincent again?"

"Yesssssss." Marlena said, rolling her eyes. "Who else?" She ran her fingers through her twist out to give her curls a little pop.

"You said he made a fool out of her, but made a fool out of who?" Donna hiccupped, disregarding the annoyed expression her best friend had on her face. "I'm going to need you to be a little more specific, hun." Her dark round eyes were glassy.

"That ole wanna be saint, Jamie." Marlena said as she splashed water against her face.

"Poor, thing." Donna laughed. She accidentally dropped her eyeliner on the floor.

13

"Oops." she said. She was still very much intoxicated and couldn't keep herself from giggling.

"Guess I need to get that." She said, leaning over to reveal her bare butt, with exception of a pink G-string, jiggling openly. She picked her cellular phone up off the counter, turning sideways to get a photo where her butt would be in clear view."

"Hold up." Marlena fussed. "Let me get in that pic. Tag me in it when you post it on Facebook."

"I got you, boo," Donna responded, popping her lips.

She reached in her purse for her selfie stick. They held each other close, almost as if they were lovers, as Donna snapped the pic. It was their signature pose that seemed to flood their timelines with likes and comments. Even though they were now approaching mid-thirties, they lived for the likes and the comments on Facebook. It made them feel like they were important.

"Yeah, she loves parading Vincent around, linking her arms through his and shit, acting like they so in love when we both know who he is truly in love with… and it definitely ain't her ole think-she-is-high-yellow-butt, either. Lil simple bitch get on my nerves." Donna laughed at her friend. "Dang, boo, you don't spare em, do you?" Marlena gave her the side-eye as they sashayed out of the lady's room.

"Spare em for what? Definitely not that lil twit. Maybe I'll spare her when she grows a brain. I mean, damn, bitch. How hard is it for you to see that he does not want you for real? I guess she wants to get her lil precious feelings hurt."

"Probably do." Donna continued laughing hard. "She is kind of cute, though." The door closed behind them when they walked out of the bathroom.

Chapter 2

Jamie held her composure inside of the stall where she heard everything that Marlena and Donna had said about her. She didn't understand those two. They always pretended like they liked her in her face. But here their two-faced selves were, dogging her behind her back. At least they thought it was behind her back. They had no idea that she was hiding out in the stall, trying to save face.

As soon as she knew the coast was clear, Jamie unlatched the door to the stall and walked out, skin clammy and pale like a ghost. She stood in the mirror, looking herself over. She usually had a little spare change on her midsection that she had the hardest time toning up. She had always been 'pleasingly plump', as her grandmother had constantly told her ever since her early teens. But now, she was at her thinnest. She felt it was time for her to do something about it. She had slanted eyes that seemed to bore a hole through the soul of anyone who dared to get close to her. That was the one thing about her that had scared most guys. Even though she took a lot off of guys, they always thought that she could see right through the bullshit that they tried to feed her and would eventually call them on it.

Over the past couple-of-weeks Jamie had heard countless rumors about her boyfriend, Vincent. They'd been together for ten months,

16

now. To her, it seemed as if their relationship was progressing the way that it should be. But just maybe she was wrong. There was only one way to find out. She reached inside her purse and pulled out her iPhone. Her eyes were sad as she dialed Vincent's number. He didn't answer. Jamie decided not to leave a message. She sat down on the bench inside of the lady's room, her mind running in several different directions. She brushed a single tear from her eye as she reflected on how she first met Vincent.

Tamyra Walker

One year ago

'Yeah, I hate when a woman call herself trying to keep me on lock. I'm a man and I will do what I damn well please. Bitches come a dime a dozen anyway, and that one I'm stuck with is getting on my nerves. I think it's time for me to explore my options... Option number one... Ole girl I've been paying attention to might be off limits to the typical guy who cares about these broads' feelings, but no one is off limits to me... Like I said, I am a man, and I will do what I damn well please'

~ Jamel Hamilton ~

~*~

Jamie stepped on the subway at 11:00 p.m. and she was crying her eyes out. She'd just caught her boyfriend, Jamel, with another woman... and not just any woman. When she crept up into his bedroom later that evening, she had found him laying between the thighs of the last person she ever expected.

Jamie had been calling Jamel off and on throughout the day. She really didn't want anything. She simply wanted to know if they could have lunch together at the park since she was finally off for the weekend. It was very rare for her to be off on the weekend. But that was the life she'd chosen when she decided to be a unit manager at Mercy Hospital. Ever since she'd become a registered nurse seven years before, she had felt as if her life was not her own, but that it belonged to the patients she took care of, instead.

Jamel rejected all her calls, finally turning the phone off after about the third call. Although Jamie was prone to be an optimist, she knew that something was not right. She could feel the nervousness bubbling in the pit of her stomach as she walked over to the window of her third-floor apartment and looked out at the beautiful city. She stood there, watching the kids play. She smiled as she witnessed a little frail girl, with the bluest eyes that she had ever seen with curly hair like Shirley Temple, come down the sliding board backward and land in the sand. *That'll be me someday when I'm the mother of Jamel's son and daughter*, she thought hopefully.

Children had been the last thing on Jamel's mind. He had no problem letting Jamie know that he didn't want any crumb snatchers messing with his income. He'd just started feeling like he was making a decent living and he didn't want to have to miss out on anything that he wanted to buy diapers for what he considered a miniature pooping machine. But Jamie thought that she could change his mind and planned to get pregnant soon after they were married. Marriage was another issue for Jamel. Jamie casually brought the conversation of marriage up during their third date.

"So." She said, taking a sip from her coconut rum, "What do you think about marriage?" Jamel smirked and sucked his teeth.

"I don't." He picked up his Corona and guzzled down the last half of it before popping the top on a second one.

"You don't do what," Jamie asked, just to be sure of what Jamel was saying to her.

I'll dumb it down for you, sweetheart, he silently thought. He licked the beer off his lips and gave Jamie the run down. "I don't think about marriage. If I want to be on lock-down, I'll go to prison." He ignored the furrows Jamie had in her eyebrows and continued talking. "There is no way on God's beautiful green earth that no woman is going to have me in cuffs."

"Hell, no." He said as if he had gotten aggravated at the thought. "Not unless we are fucking." He laughed at the last part of his statement as he took a big gulp of his second bottle of beer.

"Wow." Jamie said, taking another sip of her coconut rum. She sat the glass down on the table at the little bistro they were having dinner at, grabbed a couple of sweet potato fries, and hungrily shoved them into her mouth. She looked at Jamel with sheepish eyes. "I didn't know you looked at it like that. Marriage is a beautiful thing."

Jamel admired her beauty, as he held her gaze. Finally, he lowered his eyes to his cheesesteak sandwich. "Well, now you know." He shot back, slightly annoyed. He cut into his sandwich and stuck a forkful into his mouth. "I'm never going down that road." He said with his mouth full. "So, we shouldn't even have this discussion anymore, okay?" He stuck another forkful of cheesesteak in his mouth, grunting at how flavorful it was. He took a couple more bites before saying anything else. "I haven't been in here in a year or so. This cheesesteak tastes better than I remembered."

Jamie looked at him with glassy eyes. She half smiled as she stuffed a few more fries into her mouth. Regardless of what Jamel said, she had plans of her own. *Oh, I'll change his mind about marriage*, she thought. "He just hadn't met the right woman until he met me." She said, a little too confidently.

The chiming cuckoo clock that she'd found at a local flea market brought Jamie out of her trance. Slowly, she turned away from the window and walked over to her couch. She plopped down and picked up her cellular phone, deciding to have a long overdue conversation with her baby sister, Janna, to kill a little time and take her mind off Jamel.

"I'm in class." Janna said as she answered her sister's call. "I'll call you later." She ended the call without saying anything else.

Jamie took in a deep breath while exhaling slowly. "Well, let me see what Elaine is doing." She groaned, dialing one of her best friend's phone number.

"What's up, girl?" Elaine answered, out of breath.

"Thank God that you answered. What are you up to today?"

"I just came from working out…" Elaine fumbled all over her words, as if they were hard for her to enunciate.

"Come here, baby. Let daddy tap it for you again." A deep voice rang out in the background. Jamie shook her head.

"That must be Eli," she asked, laughing. "Girl, you two stay in the sack. You're going to wind up pregnant real soon."Elaine laughed nervously.

"Don't say that, girl. Shanna is enough. I don't need any more Bebe kids running around here, eating me out of house and home."

"I know that's right." Jamie said, cosigning with her friend. "Well, I see that you are going to be tied up for a while, so just hit me back when Eli leaves."

"Will do." Elaine said and hung up the phone.

8 hours later…

Jamie walked to Jamel's door with the meal she'd just prepared in her hands. Earlier, when she had gotten off the phone with Elaine, she decided she would cook his favorite dish of lasagna, and surprise him since she hadn't been able to get him on the phone all day. She sat the bag warmer down and pulled her key to his door out of her pocket. She entered the house quietly and went straight into the kitchen to fill a plate with some of her five-cheese lasagna. She was going to make sure he was straight first, and then she would fill up a plate for herself. They would sit out on the balcony and enjoy their meal before they retired to the bedroom for a night of passionate lovemaking.

"Oh, he is going to be so surprised." Jamie squealed as she walked up the stairs. She couldn't wait to see the look on his face when he saw the big plate of lasagna, garlic bread, and Caesar salad. She'd even brought him a slice of her homemade strawberry cheesecake.

She twisted the doorknob and walked into the master suite with a smile of anticipation on her face. Her face dropped quicker than a stroke victim's as the sounds of sexual pleasure rang out. She turned the corner and felt her chest tightening. Elaine was on top of Jamel.

"Oh yyyyeeeeah, baby." She moaned, as she held her hands firmly against his chest for better leverage. Jamel then flipped her over and covered her body with his. He lifted one of her legs and plunged himself deeply inside of her. She moaned and met him stroke for stroke. "You know how to do it, daddy. Beat it up, baby."

Elaine paused mid-stroke when she heard a pained gasp from someone else in the room. She looked up to see Jamie standing there with her eyes about to pop out of her head. She'd just got back on top of Jamel and decided to ride him backwards until they both came.

"Oh my, God," Elaine said, hopping off of Jamel's erect manhood. "What are you doing here, Jamie," she asked, shocked. She immediately grabbed for the sheets to cover her bare breasts. At the same time speckles of the sauce from the lasagna splattered on the sheets as Jamie dropped the plate on the floor. Glass shattered everywhere. She looked over and saw the Luis Vuitton overnight bag that she'd given to Elaine sitting on Jamel's chair. She knew then that Elaine had been there at least for a couple of nights.

Her eyes watered as she thought, *that was Jamel's voice I heard earlier when I was on the phone with Elaine. She lied to me. She pretended like she had been working out. The only working out she's been doing is my man.* Elaine saw Jamie looking at the bag and knew what she was thinking.

"Look, Jamie," She reasoned. "We never meant to hurt you. We were going to tell you."

"Oh, really? So, when were you going to tell me," Jamie asked, as her voice became choked up. "Before or after you two disrespectful motherfuckers came all over these satin sheets that I spent my hard earned money on?"

Elaine glanced over at Jamel for his help with explaining the situation. Jamel looked unbothered. He figured since Jamie showed up at his house uninvited, it was her fault that she saw what she saw.

Jamie looked at Jamel with tears pouring down her face. He shrugged his shoulder in response. She shook her head at him, refusing to say anything at all. As she raced out of the room and headed for the staircase, she heard Elaine scrambling to put on her robe to run after her.

"Wait, Jamie! Damn, stop being so childish and hear me out, okay." Elaine walked over to Jamie and tried to touch her. Jamie picked up the wine bottle from the table in the foyer and busted her upside the head.

"Don't touch me!" She screamed, as blood trickled down her best friend's forehead. She stood there for a few seconds breathing hard and holding her chest.

"I can't believe you laid up in here having sex with my man. Elaine rolled her eyes up in the top of her head and took a deep breath.

Tamyra Walker

"Why Elaine? What's the matter? Your fiancé, Eli, who you claim to love so much is not enough for you?" She didn't bother to wipe away the tears that ran down her cheeks to freedom. Elaine simply glared at her, not knowing what to say. Honestly, she wasn't sorry, either.

"What the hell was that?" Jamel asked. He came to the top of the staircase wearing a pair of polo boxer briefs. More tears fell from Jamie's face, as she watched her boyfriend staring at her friend like he cared more about her. She ran out the door, sobbing harder than she did when she'd heard the news about the untimely passing of her father.

But she didn't have time to be in the bed with heartache. Jamel had shown her exactly how cold and calculating he was. And he didn't give a single care about how painful it was to her. There was nothing more for her to than tuck her tail between her legs and move on. Two months later, she was in a relationship with Vincent Hargrove, a guy who she didn't know and who would only birth more pain in her heart.

Chapter 3

'I guess you can call me a G. I'm like the rapper, Ludacris, I got hoes in different area codes. As long as they flock to me, like a herd of lost sheep I feel compelled to give them what I know they want, but this one right here... that cutie sitting over there, yeah she's different. She's going to be an upgrade to my resume'

~ Vincent Hargrove ~

~*~

Vincent walked up to Jamie as she sat on the subway, blinded by her tears, after catching her boyfriend, Jamel, in bed with her best friend, Elaine.

He gazed upon her with awe from the other end of the subway before he got the nerve to walk up to her. He knew that type of cry, anywhere. Baby girl was heartbroken. He knew that she was crying over a man, and he either had to have dumped her or she found him laying with somebody else.

"Wipe those tears, beautiful." He whispered to her and handed her a Kleenex.

Jamie grabbed the Kleenex out of Vincent's hands and wiped her face. She looked up to meet his gaze. He was handsome enough. His complexion seemed to be as sweet as caramel dripping off of a candy apple. Melanin was definitely his best friend. He wore a low haircut, and had the body of a professional trainer. In fact, she'd never seen a guy before whose torso was as defined as his.

"I know you are hurting." He said handing her another Kleenex. "It's written all over your pretty little face."

Jamie didn't say anything. She continued dabbing at the tears that was running down her chestnut colored face.

"Here is my number." He said, handing her one of his business cards. "When you pull yourself together and are ready for a real man who is going to spoil you and treat you like a queen- call me. I got you. And I promise I will never make you cry."

Vincent was outdoing himself. He was as confident as they came, but he'd never came across as cocky like he was acting now. He figured he had to be blunt with her. She didn't look like the type to fall for the okeydokey.

Jamie looked up to meet his eyes again. She sucked her teeth and gave him a, 'yeah-right-you-are-just-like-the-rest-of-them' expression.

"Give me a chance, sweetheart. What could be so bad about us getting to know each other?" Vincent knew what she was thinking and wanted to plead his case. "I'm not the sorry excuse for a man that made you cry. I want you to see that for yourself."

"Please leave me alone." Jamie barely got her words out, as she was once more sobbing. Vincent reached down, taking his finger and gently placing it on Jamie's face. He wiped the tears away. "Much better." He said, slowly backing away. "I'm sorry for your pain. Please use that number."

Tamyra Walker

Two days later...

Jamie pulled up in her truck on Harrison Court and got out. She immediately activated the alarm as she walked up the sidewalk to the condos that were before her. Azalea Springs was a decent neighborhood. The houses weren't run down and the schools were okay. Still, Jamie was guarded. She wasn't taking a chance. There had been a couple of suspicious things going on that made her raise her eye.

"Where is 1801-C?" She mumbled. "Oh, here." She said, as she walked up to the door and raised her hand to knock. To say she was nervous was an understatement. "I'm going straight to hell on a Ferry for this." She said as she allowed her hand to make contact with the door. Just as she raised her hand to knock a second time, the person she was looking for opened the door.

"Whoa, what a pleasant surprise." he said. he took a couple of steps back. "I thought I had given you my number in vain."

Jamie was speechless as Vincent stood before her in sweats and a wife beater. He smiled, "Yeah I know you like what you see. I worked hard for these gains."

Jamie's thoughts were on a rampage. Her mouth began to water. *Jesus Christ, he is fiiiiiine*!

"Can I come in," she finally asked, shifting uncomfortably as he loomed over her like a God.

"Well, I was about to go to the gym. But that can wait. Sure, come on in, boo." He moved over to the side so that Jamie could accompany him. Her nipples instantly became hard as her breasts grazed Vincent's perfectly chiseled chest. "Can I get you something?" He asked. "I've got Pepsi, bottled water, and wine. I bet you would love a glass of wine."

Jamie walked into Vincent's space and sat down on the futon. His condo was truly a mancave. Pictures of Muhammed Ali adorned the walls. There was a Harley Davidson sitting in the dining room, along with a bench press and different size barbells.

"Isn't she gorgeous?" Vincent asked, as he saw Jamie staring at his bike. "That's my sweetheart, Nikki. We've been riding together for about five years. Every chance I get, I fix her up... add a little more bells and whistles. You know what I'm saying?"

"She is a beauty." Jamie agreed.

"Soooooo, what brings you this way?" He walked into the kitchen and put several cubes of ice in a glass. He opened the Pepsi, listening to it fizz before pouring Jamie a glass, placing it on the countertop, and then pouring himself a glass.

"Here you go, pretty lady." Vincent said.

Jamie took the glass out of his hand, smiling nervously. Vincent turned his up, draining the glass.

"Pepsi is always, refreshing."

Jamie didn't respond. She averted her attention to Vincent and said.

"Yes, you can get me something, but Pepsi is not what I want."

"Wine." Vincent asked, standing and walking toward his wine cabinet.

Jamie cleared her throat.

"You can get me you."

Vincent laughed at Jamie's boldness.

"Come again?" He said.

Jamie looked at him without flinching. She knew that she may have shocked him because she beat him to the punch of asking him for what he was eventually going to ask her for. But she didn't have time to stroke his bruised ego, when she wanted him to stroke her, right there on his futon. They were both adults. So, there was no need to be modest.

"Come again?" He said again, chuckling lightly.

"Look. Will you fuck me, please?" Jamie asked, as she stood next to him and slid out of her dress.

"Wow, ma. Well, I guess you do know what you want," Vincent said as he started to fiddle with the buttons on his shirt. Jamie didn't respond. He walked towards her, trying to kiss her. She put her hand up to stop him.

"Save the sentimental crap for your woman I know you got. I just want you to fuck me… hard. Can you do that for me, please?"

"What makes you think I have a woman? I can be all yours, if you want me."

Jamie rolled her eyes up in her head.

"If you say anything else, I'm just going to leave. Please save the lies, okay. Now I came here to fuck. Are you going to fuck me or not?"

"Your wish is my command." Vincent said, grabbing her and pulling her towards him. She slapped his hand away, turned around and leaned over the futon.

"I want it from the back."

Chapter 4

"Dammit, I'm going to be late for work again, for the second day this week. Lord, please don't let me get written up." Jamie rolled over in Vincent's bed and looked at the digital alarm clock sitting on his night table. "That can't be right." She said, leaning closer to make sure that her eyes weren't playing tricks on her. She couldn't believe that it was 6:25 a.m. already. It seemed as if she had only gone to sleep about an hour earlier. The last thing she wanted to do was go to work where she had to deal with unhappy family members and disgruntled employees who thought that just because she was their boss she was equivalent to God. More than anything, she wanted to lay, tangled in the sheets on Vincent's bed. They were dampened with his sweat and seeds of love. And why shouldn't they be when they'd gone three rounds last night before finally collapsing on their backs, falling asleep in each other's arms. Jamie smiled. She closed her eyes and allowed her mind to take her back a few hours.

She had walked in Vincent's condo at 6 p.m., sashayed over to him where he was sitting in his gaming chair, playing a game of Madden, leaned over, and kissed him quickly on the lips.

"How was your day?" He asked, looking up to note her butt in her scrubs as she kicked off her Alegria work shoes, placing them and her work bag in the hall closet.

"Stressful." She said, taking a deep breath as she thought about the two patients who'd coded in the ICU where she was the boss.

One had had a massive heart attack. They got him to the Cath lab just in time for his heart to explode. He didn't make it. The other patient, was an eighteen-year-old asthmatic. She was promptly intubated and would be lucky if she made it through the night. Her name was Melanie. She'd promised Jamie when she was in ICU four months prior that she was going to quit smoking. Of course she didn't stop.

Jamie shook her head to keep the thought of that young girl possibly dying from plaguing her mind.

"And why are you looking at my butt, sir?" She asked with a devilish smile emerging in the corner of her lips.

Vincent shrugged his shoulders.

"It's kind of out there, boo. Can't help but to notice it." He said making a slapping sound with his mouth. Jamie looked at him with her eyes crossed.

Tamyra Walker

"You're too funny." She said tossing a throw pillow at his head. She walked into the kitchen and began to ransack the cabinets. "I'm going to get dinner started. Anything in particular you want?"

"You got it," Vincent responded, still gazing longingly at her butt. "Do your thing." Jamie shook her head, smiling to herself.

"All right, then. I'll hook something up for you."

Vincent didn't say anything. He gave her a nod of approval and went back to playing his game. He didn't have the traditional mother who would put her apron on with grace, standing in the kitchen for hours cooking up fattening meals. No, his mother, Greta, made him and his sister, Malina, fend for themselves at an early age. They weren't even allowed to call her 'mother'. She had ordered them to call her by her first name. And, she felt that if they were hungry enough, they knew how to go into the kitchen and fry themselves a piece of bologna or boil a hotdog. There was always plenty of cereal that she stocked up on from the local food banks that they could have for breakfast.

Vincent wasn't used to getting a hot meal at least every other day. So, he was feeling like a king on the throne since Jamie didn't mind showing off her cooking skills. She sat in his living room on the futon with her feet tucked under her legs while he stood at the counter in the kitchen eating like he hadn't had a good home cooked meal in a month of Sundays. He sopped the gravy off his fingers, from the smothered pork chops, washed his hands in the kitchen sink, and rushed over to Jamie's side, picking her up in one big swoop.

"Where you taking me?" She asked seductively, dropping the magazine that she was browsing on the floor. She knew all along that she'd be stripped down to her black lace Victoria secret's push up bra and boy shorts in less than five minutes.

"You'll see." Vincent said, as he carried her into his bedroom and gently placed her atop the bed. He walked over to his dresser and hit play on his stereo system. Teddy Pendergrass's, grown sexy voice began to sing Turn off the lights.

"That's just what I'm about to do, too." Vincent said as he dimmed the lights in his bedroom.

"You're a bad boy." Jamie poked her lips out like she was pouting.

"Well, I guess you better send me to detention, then." Vincent shot back as he unbuckled his belt and jeans. He let them fall to his ankles and Jamie's mouth dropped wide open when she saw his beautiful soldier saluting her at perfect attention.

"Look a dere." She whispered as he pressed his rock hard body against hers. She squirmed under his weight as he planted passionate

kisses all over her body, thinking to herself, I can't wait to feel every inch of you.

"Ummmmmmm. Your lips feel so good." She moaned, between kisses. "I wish we could be like this forever, baby. You make me feel so complete."

"Who taught you how to cook like that?" Vincent asked. "That's old-school cooking girl." He wasn't about to have the "love" discussion with Jamie that she was trying to have. He already knew she could only be in love with how he was putting it on her. There was no possible way she could be in love with him that quickly. He started to wonder just how quickly she had moved with Jamel, her ex-boyfriend, in the first place and how many other guys had she moved this quickly with. He tried hard not to think about how she came to his house the first night they had sex and threw it at him like it had an expiration date on it. Most of his side-chicks were in their feelings about him only wanting to have sex and not actually hanging out with them. But Jamie didn't want that. Sure, he wanted to have sex with her. He knew that the first moment he laid eyes on her. However, he couldn't deny that she had thrown him through a loop with how forward she was. It was hard for him to see past that now that she was obviously trying to show him she was a good girl.

Jamie sneaked one more peck on Vincent's lips. "Well, I used to watch my mother cook when I was little. She and grandma participated in cooking contests all the time. They always won at least second place. Most times it was first place. When I turned about seven or eight, I pretended like I was running my own restaurant. I had already written down all my favorite recipes from my grandmother's and mother's kitchen. My dolls were my customers..." Jamie paused to note the expression on Vincent's face. She could only hope she wasn't rambling on, boring him to pieces.

He had his eyes closed, gently running his fingers across her cheek.

"That tickles." She giggled, pushing his hand away.

"Oh, yeah," Vincent said.

He cupped her breasts in his hands and placed his lips over hers. He kissed her gently, but passionately, deepening the kiss when he felt Jamie's body reacting accordingly. Slowly, he moved down to her hardened nipples and sucked them like he was a newborn baby feasting on his mother's breast milk.

Jamie held her lips like she would if she were blowing out candles on a birthday cake. She arched her back and let out a loud gasp when Vincent moved down to her navel and even further down to her forbidden fruit. He skillfully ran his tongue over her, like it was finding

39

its way through a maze. He held her in place when she tried to get away.

"Where you think you going?" He asked looking up to meet her tear streaked face. "You can't run away from this."

"I can't take it baby." She huffed. Vincent pushed her legs back and held her tighter as he continued kissing her in her most intimate spot.

"Make love to me, now." She whimpered.

Vincent looked at her and smiled. He had her right where he wanted her. Her eyes pleaded with his to enter her and he obliged, entering her body slowly. Jamie reached up and tried to pull him further into her as she sunk her fingernails into his back.

"Ohhhhhhhh." She said, as he started off stroking her slowly.

"You like that, don't you?" Vincent asked in a low tone. He gently grabbed Jamie's face and made her look at him. "Answer me." He said, speeding up his pace just a little.

"I lo... loove it baby." Jamie stuttered, as she held onto him. Tears of pleasure ran down both of her cheeks. "Pl...please, don't stop. Oooooh baby, yeah baby!"

Vincent placed both of his hands under her buttocks and raised her up to him. He slid in and out of Jamie until she was panting and screaming almost uncontrollably, shuddering like she was having chills.

Beep... beep... Beep. The alarm clock finally went off, interrupting Jamie's thoughts. She opened her eyes and wiped the sweat that was starting to accumulate on her forehead. Reminiscing about last night had gotten her ready for an encore. But she would have to wait until tonight, or maybe she could sneak in a little quickie on her lunch break. She sighed heavily as she threw the sheets off her and stood up. She stretched and yawned noisily, dragging her feet over to Vincent's Chester drawer to find herself a clean pair of scrubs.

"Well, good morning, beautiful." Vincent adored Jamie when she walked into the bathroom and turned on the shower. He stood, butt naked in front of the mirror, brushing his teeth.

"See, that's why I'm going to be late again this morning." Jamie teased. "You and that beautiful body of yours. I can't seem to get enough."

"Oh, baby, you ain't seen nothing yet. I got plenty more for you." He flexed his muscles, undoubtedly thinking he was the man.

"Um hummm." I bet you do, baby. "Too bad I can't see right now. I got to get to work before I don't have a job anymore." She allowed the towel that covered her nakedness to hit the floor. As she turned to get into the shower, Vincent smacked her on the butt.

"Yeah, all of that is mine," he said.

"Yeah, it's all yours as long as you are treating me right." Jamie remarked, pulling the curtain. Vincent rolled his eyes and walked out of the bathroom. Jamie lathered her body up with pomegranate dove body wash. The loofah felt good against her skin. She smiled to herself thinking, *I'd like to have Vincent's babies. Hell, I'd like to be his wife. At the rate we are going I know it won't be long before he put a ring on it.*

Ten minutes later, just as Jamie turned off the shower and stepped out to dry off, she heard Vincent on the phone, talking in a hushed tone.

"Look, I'll call you later, aight? No… no… hell no, you cannot come over. Ju..just give me about an hour, okay? I'll be over there. I promise. Yeah… I… look. I gotta go. Bye."

Jamie walked into the bedroom and sat down on the corner of the bed.

Vincent looked at her nervously.

"Dang, boo. That's the shortest shower you have ever taken. You really think you are going to be late, huh?"

"I'm sure everything will be okay, babe." Jamie said. Vincent couldn't help noticing how cool her voice had become. "Wh…who, was that on the phone?" She asked, sticking her fingers down in her jar of coconut oil and rubbing it on her legs. She tried her best not to sound concerned. But even Ray Charles could've seen that she was bothered.

Vincent felt his anger rising to the surface. *I know damn well she didn't just ask me who was on my phone that I pay the bill on every month. None of her business. If I wanted her to know I would just tell her without her asking me. See, I know now her lil catty behind is trying to start some mess.*

"I made you an omelet." Vincent responded, totally ignoring the question Jamie had asked him. "Come on, you need to get going." He said laughing, almost pushing her to the front door when she put her lab jacket on and placed her lanyard with her ID badge around her neck. He wasn't very gentle about it. He handed her the cheese omelet that he had placed in one of her small Tupperware containers. *Bitch, get your nosy self out of my house before I put my foot up your behind,* he thought.

Jamie walked out into the brisk cool air, feeling frustrated. She knew that Vincent had heard her question. She also knew that he deliberately did not answer it.

She and Vincent had been together for one month now. Ever since that first day she walked into his home for a rendezvous to take her mind off Jamel, she knew that she had to have him whenever she wanted. He had been too good in bed for her to let him slip through her fingers and have another woman singing the five octaves he had always had her singing whenever he was deep inside of her. She tried not to catch feelings for him. She tried to convince herself that it was nothing more than good sex, which truly was the case for Vincent. But he had her fooled. He knew when he first saw her crying on that subway that he was going to sex the daylights out of her. If she was any good, he would hit it twice. And if she played her cards right- he'd make her one of his top side chicks. She could never be number one, because the number one slot was already taken.

Alese, his woman of five years would be coming home from basic training from the Air-force in just a little over two weeks. He had no intentions of getting rid of Jamie. He had good use for her. But she was going to have to start back staying in her own apartment. Alese wasn't going to live with him either. Still, she was known to just pop up randomly. When she did, he didn't want to have to explain why another woman was at his house.

Chapter 5

Vincent was careful not to break any of Jamie's perfumes as he placed them all in a box next to the two duffle bags with all her clothes that were in his closet and drawers. He walked, long steps, back to his room to do one fuller search. He scanned the room carefully as if he was a detective looking for evidence in a murder case. He wanted to make sure that he hadn't forgotten anything that belonged to her. He figured that if he hurried up and packed her things he could just load it up in his F-150 and drop it off at her apartment. He would then return her key. He wasn't officially breaking up with her, just yet, but if he started cutting her off now, she would be use to the idea of them not spending so much time together when Alese touched down.

He planned to propose to Alese on her birthday, when they were alone together on their trip to Dubai that he had planned for them a couple of months ago. Alese had proven herself worthy, and though she had ghetto tendencies, since she had grown up in one of the most notorious projects in Charlotte, North Carolina, but she wasn't always nagging him like all the girls he dealt with in the past- including the ones from the suburbs and the upscale neighborhoods. And she didn't use the fact that she had grown up in the hood, to stay in the hood and not try to be anything in life. Sure, she had gotten a late start. She'd delved into drama for a while, but she knew that she had to grow up. Her friend, Angelica, was gunned down in the same projects that they grew up in over a man that wanted any and everyone who was willing to splurge on him. That had been her wake up call.

Vincent placed Jamie's diamond stud earrings and Rolex watch that her grandmother had given to her in the box with her perfumes. He walked back in his room and spotted her nude teddy across his recliner.

"Now, I could watch her pop that ass in this again!" He said, grinning, lying across the bed, sniffing the crotch of the teddy. His eyes then averted to the small hole on the wall over his headboard.

"Yeah, I was banging it so hard I knocked a damn hole in the wall. I ought not fix that shit. Ought to just let it be a reminder of how supreme her loving is. But of course, Alese, will want to know how it got there and why I haven't attempted to get it fixed."

A loud, staccato knock on his door startled him. As he sat up on the side of the bed, he heard someone attempting to unlock his door.

"That's her now." Vincent said aloud, disappointed that he hadn't started packing her things earlier. He closed his night table drawer he'd just opened to retrieve his pistol. At first, he thought it might have been a prowler at his door. He quickly dismissed that idea when he heard Jamie's voice. Taking a deep breath, he walked over to the bay window in his living room. He peeked out the blinds just to be sure. Jamie stood there with a confused expression on her face. She was jimmying the key in the lock, still trying to unlock the door. Vincent stared at her a few seconds before he lightly tapped on the window and signaled to her that he was coming to the door.

"What's wrong with my key, babe?" Jamie asked, leaning over to kiss Vincent as soon as he opened the door. He allowed their lips to touch briefly before he grabbed Jamie by the hand, pulling her in the house and gently closing the door.

"Ouch!" She yelled out in pain as she tripped over something, twisting her ankle. She looked down to see that it was a duffle bag.

Jamie put both of her hands up and shrugged her shoulders. "Are we having company, baby?"

Vincent looked slightly nervous. He scratched the top of his head, the way he always did when he was feeling kind of uncertain. There was nothing Jamie could do to change his mind about her leaving his house. But he didn't want to be overly brutal in the process. She could cause trouble for him and Alese. That was the last thing that he wanted. He'd already promised Alese that he would never mess around on her again after a video was leaked of him having sex with Brenesha Thomas in the shower room at the gym. Alese had slept with

Brenesha's boyfriend, Ahmad, back in the tenth grade. She'd been holding a grudge against her ever since.

"I'll pay your ass back, bitch." She warned Alese, with tears of hurt and shame rolling down her cheeks. She did just that when she deliberately joined the gym that Vincent worked at. She set the whole shenanigan up for him to sleep with her and then had the gall to send the tape to Alese for Christmas that year. There was a note inside that read, "Now that's karma for you! Lol."

Vincent sighed heavily as he thought about all the drama that Brenesha had caused. Alese had flattened all his tires on his truck-twice, and keyed his Crown Victoria. But that wasn't enough to satisfy her hunger for revenge. She broke into his house and ripped up all his furniture and spray painted, 'Dog ass nigga' on his dining room table. That's why he didn't have one when Jamie started coming over. But despite how angry Alese was, she eventually gave him another chance. He had been very careful ever since to not get caught with his pants down. He tried hard not to cheat. But there were just too many easy women he dealt with, who were willing to give it up without him having to even do anything for it. And why should he be faithful anyway when he'd always seen his uncles cheating on their wives. Most of them had good women. Still, they had to have something extra. It seemed to be cruel and unusual punishment for them to settle for only laying between the thighs of the one who graciously took their last name.

Jamie asked him again,

"Are we having company, honey?"

"Not exactly, sweetie," Vincent finally responded.

"Well, whose things are these?" Jamie walked over to survey the pile of stuff more carefully.

"Is that my watch?" She asked. The box with it and her jewelry had fallen over when she tripped over the duffle bag.

"Come sit on the couch with me and let's talk Jamie." Vincent patted the spot next to him on the futon.

"I don't need to sit down, Vincent. Just tell me what is going on. Since that is my jewelry, I'm assuming those must be my clothes in the duffle bags. Are you trying to tell me something?" Jamie stood in front of Vincent with her arms folded. She was so confused. She and Vincent had just made love that morning. She had decided since she didn't have to go to work until 9 she would cook him breakfast. She stood in the kitchen wearing her sheer negligee that Vincent had bought her, scrambling eggs, and frying sausage. The grits were cooking slowly. The ingredients for the cinnamon French toast was laid out on the counter as well. Jamie walked over to the refrigerator and removed the jug of Tropicana orange juice.

"Ah hem." Vincent said as he walked into the kitchen and grabbed her from behind. He'd stood in the doorway watching for several long minutes. *She's not wearing any panties*, he thought, instantly feeling a bulge in his silk boxers.

"Oh, hey boo." Jamie turned around to smile at him.

"Let's try out this new dining room table you convinced me to get, baby." He whispered, sticking his tongue in her ear long enough to make her shudder. He then planted a wet kiss on the back of her neck.

"Okay, let me put the food on the table, honey."

Vincent smiled and picked her up, throwing her across his shoulder and smacking her hard on the butt.

"I think that there's been a slight misunderstanding, Jamie. I want you on the table. Forget them damn eggs. You're what I want for breakfast. You dig?"

"Oh, you are really bad." Jamie said as she wrapped her legs around his neck and positioned herself on the table to be Vincent's meal. They'd made so much noise that Vincent's neighbor who worked the night shift and slept during the day had to bang on the wall.

"Damn, dude! Can you two please do something besides have sex all times of the day?" He asked, very much annoyed.

Jamie couldn't understand what could have happened so suddenly that he would pack up her things. And then her mouth dropped open and she walked up closer to Vincent's face. "Is that why my key wouldn't work? Did you change the locks on me?" She didn't have to wait for him to respond. She already knew the answer. Immediately her eyes welled up with tears.

"So, this... we..." She said, pointing from him to her, "It was all fun and games for you, huh?" Her voice started to tremble as a tear rolled down her cheek.

Here she goes, with that crying shit, he thought.

"What are you talking about, girl?" Vincent placed his hands across his chest like he was shocked. It would make it easier for him if she was willing to forget all about him. But since she hadn't done anything but be sweet to him, he wasn't going to suggest that. "I'm not breaking up with you... I...I mean, you don't want to break up with me, do you?"

"So, why is my stuff packed, Vincent?" Jamie sniffed, pointing her hand in the direction of her belongings. "Why did you change the locks?"

Tamyra Walker

"We…we…well, I was meaning to tell you that my next-door neighbors said someone was snooping by my door. I figured it might've been an ex who still had a key, baby. That's why I changed the locks, so I wouldn't have to worry about it."

Jamie looked at him with a 'motherfucker-I-know-your-ass-is-lying' expression on her face. But she kept quiet and just stared at him.

"Oh, so you think I'm bullshitting, huh? Is that it?" Vincent turned to walk away. He couldn't bear to look Jamie in her eyes that moment. She was making him feel weak. And the last thing he liked was to feel weak.

Maaaaaan, I ain't up for this interrogation now. Shit, she acting like she my wife or something. She ain't got to go home if she doesn't want to. But she is getting the hell away from here. See, that's why I don't do broads up in my space, got me acting soft.

"Jamie," Vincent groaned, trying hard not to sound aggravated. "Let's try this again, boo. We. Are. Not. Breaking. Up. Okay." He said it slowly. "The truth of the matter is I need a little space. I mean, you have been here…"

"Because you wanted me here." Jamie interrupted. She had a 'no-you-didn't-go-there' expression woven into her features now.

"Don't interrupt me, dammit." Vincent raised his voice just slightly.

Jamie didn't say anything. She stood there, crying still, mad at herself for even acknowledging him that day on the subway.

"Now. Like I said-" He continued talking with his voice elevated. "We are not breaking up. I need space. I never intended for you to move up in here."

Again, Jamie's mouth flew open and the tears began to flow more rapidly. She couldn't believe Vincent had said that to her.

"Well, then." She said, barely audible. "I'll just move out. How about that?" She turned away from him and began to pick up her bags. Vincent walked over to help her.

"Put my shit down. Now. I don't need your help." The fact he tried to help her offended her even more. He must've been unable to wait for her to leave his place! She walked out of the door with two of the bags, used her keyless remote to open her trunk, and threw the bags in with as much attitude as she could muster. When she walked back into the house, Vincent stood before her naked. She placed her hand over her chest, shocked.

"Now, look." Vincent spoke. "I told your stubborn ass that I'm not breaking up with you. You ain't leaving here with that attitude. So,

I guess I'm just going to have to put all of this on you until I see a smile emerge on that pretty lil face of yours."

He stretched out his hand and reached for her. She didn't budge. She stood still, a new set of tears rolling down her face.

Vincent sucked his teeth.

"Girl, you know you want this. Stop acting and come on over here and get it." Jamie walked over to him and pushed him down on the couch hard. She undressed, climbed on top of him, turned his face so that he could look directly in her eyes, and slapped him as hard as she could.

"You asshole." She angrily said.

"You're going to pay for that." Vincent said as he grabbed her and threw her off him. He pushed her face down into the couch. It wasn't long before her sobs of hurt had turned into screams of pleasure.

"Do you mind if I wash up?" She asked afterwards. He tried to hold onto her. But she was still mad at him, even though her body had rejected how she sincerely felt.

"You know that you can." Vincent loosened his grip. Jamie stood. He slapped her on the butt just to see it jiggle while she walked to the bathroom. She shot him a cold glare in response.

"Don't be looking at me like that. We have already established that all of that is mine." He said, closing his eyes, placing his hands behind his head. Five minutes later he was snoring lightly. He woke a couple hours later to Jamie cooking porterhouse steak, asparagus and loaded baked potatoes.

"Now that smells good." He mumbled, heading in the direction of the bathroom so he could shower. He decided he could use another round of loving. So, he wasn't going to make Jamie leave that day.

Tamyra Walker

Chapter 6

Several months later…

"If I don't get to this bathroom now, I am going to pee on myself." A slight tinge of urgency was in Jamie's voice as she left the dance floor at Ayanna's birthday party in a flash. She had been enjoying Joe's crooning for the last hour or so. He sung all her favorite songs, including, 'Good girls.' She wanted to continue standing there listening to his beautiful voice. But her bladder was about to burst.

"Lord, please don't let me pee, on myself." She whimpered, patting her feet, anxiously trying to get her brown leather leggings down that she ordered from Nordstrom's online store. She wore a leopard printed blouse with a pair of small hooped earrings. Her slightly coarse hair was pulled up into a spiral ponytail, accentuated with a leopard print scarf she wore as a headband. Her three-inch clogs went perfectly with her outfit. And she beat her face like she had never done before with the Mary Kay makeup that she'd ordered from her sister, Janna.

The bathroom door creaked open. The air was immediately filled with the stench of self-centeredness. Jamie could hear whoever it was heels on the tiled floor. And then the mysterious person spoke.

"Get your drunk ass in here and pull yourself together, bitch." Marlena snapped.

Jamie froze in place. She would know those two ratchet voices anywhere. Marlena and Donna, Vincent's best friends ever since Elementary school had just walked into the bathroom. The party floor where they'd been gyrating on every man that gave them a second stare wasn't big enough for the three of them. This less than 1,000-square-foot bathroom for sure wasn't going to be able to contain all three of their attitudes within its walls. Jamie sat as quietly as she could on the commode, refusing to even finish emptying her bladder for fear they would wait until she came out of the stall to see who was eavesdropping on their conversation. She didn't want to run into those two, ever. It was just something about them that didn't sit well with her. For one, they were more plastic than the thermos in a lunchbox, and she was already feeling slightly queasy from the Mexican dip she'd just eaten about a half hour-ago. That and the constant running to the bathroom, seemingly every other hour was enough for her. Marlena and Donna would push her beyond insanity with their over the top petty behavior. While sitting there, she couldn't help recounting the first time they met.

It was five months ago. Jamie was finally starting to get used to staying back in her apartment. She'd gone out to dinner with her sister the night before to celebrate her sisterhood into the AKA sorority.

Tamyra Walker

Janna's voice was filled with so much glee when she called Jamie a couple hours before. She answered the phone, half way expecting it to be Vincent.

"What's up, sis?" Janna spoke before Jamie could say anything.

"Oh, it's you." Jamie jokingly said.

"Yeah, it's me, big sis. I'm going to get you for that comment another day, but I need you to get your butt up off the sofa or the bed and come chill with me and my girls tonight. I'm not taking no for an answer, either. Ciao."

Jamie blew hard and placed the phone back on the table. Janna had hung up without saying anything else. "Well, I guess it won't hurt to hang out a bit." She said, standing to find something to wear. Now that she was well rested from a night of chilling with her sister and her friends, she decided she would spend the day being a homebody. Janna had gotten too intoxicated and slept overnight on her sister's loveseat. She'd just peeled herself off the sofa a couple hours before, drank two cups of coffee, and dragged her feet out the door where her new boo, Pernell, was waiting on her. "I'll call you later." She said to Jamie as she left.

Jamie was sitting on her chaise, watching Fatal Attraction for the umpteenth time on lifetime movie network, while sipping a virgin strawberry daiquiri that she'd made herself. The doorbell chimed a half hour later, startling her from her flick.

Wonder who that could be? She thought, leaning forward, and placing the remote control on the coffee table. She stood and sat her daiquiri on one of the coasters next to the remote control. She caught a glimpse of herself in the mirror over her couch and decided to pull the bonnet off her head before she went to the door. She peeped through the peephole after pretty much sprinting to the door. A confused expression colored her face as she opened the door.

"I thought you'd be doing a few classes at the gym today." She said to Vincent.

"Does that mean you're not happy to see me?" Vincent asked. "Dang, boo can I get a kiss?"

"Sure, you can, baby," Jamie cooed and planted a wet one on his lips. "I didn't say I wasn't happy to see you. Of course, I'm happy to see you. I just..."

Suddenly, two ladies emerged from Vincent's truck and slammed the door. They sashayed up the driveway, twisting extra hard, wearing questionable attire.

"Who are they?" Jamie asked, her eyes widened. Her heart was doing somersaults in her chest, as she knew that Vincent hadn't had

59

the nerve to bring some chicks he was messing around with to her home.

Vincent smiled, flattered by her obvious jealousy.

"Oh, baby. You're going to love them. That's Marlena and Donna. We have been best friends since the third grade…"

"Second grade." Donna interrupted with much attitude. Her eyes were fastened on Jamie. She looked over at Marlena, who had a smirk on her face. She was also staring at Jamie, almost through her.

"Vincent, noooooo you didn't!" Jamie yelled, nudging him playfully. "Why didn't you call first and tell me you were bringing your friend's over? I would've put on some clothes. You got me meeting them in these ole frumpy cookie monster pajama bottoms."

"Cut all of that out… you know you fine, boo." Vincent reached out and groped Jamie right there in front of his friends.

"Stop it, boy," she squealed, embarrassed. She slapped his hand away and looked at him with a 'why-are-you-showing-out' expression on her face.

Vincent looked over at Marlena and Donna.

"Isn't my baby fine?"

"If you say so." Donna had blurted out before she could stop herself. Marlena slapped her on the arm.

"Of course, she is." She stuttered, trying to clean up the mess her friend had made. She sneaked a glance at Donna and they both began snickering.

Jamie rolled her eyes at the thought of those two, as she sat, still trapped in the stall.

"Yeah, she loves parading Vincent around, linking her arm through his and shit, acting like they so in love when we both know who he is truly in love with... and it definitely ain't her ole think-she-is-high-yellow-butt, either. Lil simple bitch get on my damn nerves."

Jamie's thoughts were interrupted when Marlena spoke again. She and Donna had just taken a selfie and resumed talking about her. She placed both of her hands over her mouth to stifle the gasp wanting to spew out that very moment.

What do they mean I'm not the one who Vincent is truly in love with? Suddenly, it seemed as if the walls were closing in on her. If Marlena and Donna didn't hurry up and leave, she would have to reveal herself.

She was starting to feel dizzy and didn't know how much longer she could stand. Sweat began to pour out of her pores as she willed herself to stop listening to Marlena and Donna. Thankfully, she calmed herself down, until she heard the door to the bathroom open.

"I guess she wants to get her lil precious feelings hurt."

"Probably do." Donna continued laughing hard, as the door closed behind her.

"She is kind of cute, though."

Jamie and Vincent didn't hang out nearly as much as they did in the beginning of their relationship. But she was giving him his space. She missed him, would give up her apartment in a heartbeat if he asked her to come live with him, or he could give up his condo to come live with her. She would even foot most of the bills since she made double what he made as a Registered nurse with a master's degree. In fact, she was only a few credits shy of obtaining her degree to be a nurse practitioner. She didn't want to live off Vincent. She could take care of herself. She just wanted him to be her man. But it was obvious that he wanted them to be married before they continued cohabitating. That's what he had told her. They could have sex, seven days a week. He'd even gone slightly crazy when Jamie was acting like she wasn't going to give it up to him anymore.

"If I can't get it, you must be giving it to someone else!" He'd yelled at her one afternoon, storming through her apartment and slamming doors. He'd called Jamie a couple nights before because he was feeling horny and wanted to get off, but she had ignored his phone call. A few nights later, he let himself into her apartment. He lay naked in her bed when she got out the shower. She rolled her eyes at him and began to towel dry her hair.

"I don't know what you came over here for, but I'm not in the mood Vincent. So you might as well put your dick up and scurry on over to your house that you don't want me to come to anymore." They hadn't been intimate in his home since they'd had that big fight some months back about him changing the locks on her. Every time she hinted around about coming over to his place he quickly changed the subject.

"You act like you don't want me over to your place anymore," Jamie solemnly said after about the third time he shut her down.

"Now, here you go…" He said, copping an attitude.

"Look, Vincent, I don't want this to be an argument. I'm just making an observation."

He took a deep breath.

"Dammit, Jamie, your observation is wrong. I've been busy. My clientele is growing more and more every day. You know that."

"Yeah, right Vincent." Jamie dismissed the conversation. "You're never too busy to come over here and lay up whenever you get the urge." She said and silently thought, *But, I'm going to fix you.* Since Vincent wasn't trying to understand how she felt, she would simply withhold the cookie from him. She was certain then he would get his act together if he really wanted her the way he always tried to make her believe. But he'd actually held it together better than she had. After one week of celibacy she was calling him, begging him to come and set her straight. The vibrator just wasn't hitting it for her. She wanted his hardness in her. She wanted him to grab a handful of her butt and squeeze tightly while he was making her cum.

"Oh, so you want it now, huh?" Vincent asked, laughing. "Y'all kill me playing these lil withholding games. You know this beast too good for you to be holding out on, girl."

There was only one sure way for Jamie to find out if all was as good as she thought it was. She would call Vincent up and see. He didn't answer the phone. In fact, he rejected her call.

After wiping the tear that had escaped down her cheek she stood at last and reached in her purse for the small applicator she had put in there when she was relieving her bladder. There were two very clear blue lines on the applicator.

"I knew it." She said, as more tears ran down her face. "I'm pregnant… with Vincent's child." Her hands quivered uncontrollably as she wrapped the positive pregnancy test in a paper towel and gently placed it back inside of her purse. She took a few deep breaths, squared her shoulders, and walked out the bathroom.

The next day…

Teresa walked in Jamie's bedroom and opened the curtains, allowing the sun to shine through her room.

"Why'd you do that, girl?" Jamie moaned throwing her pillow over her head.

"No. The question is why have you been rejecting my phone calls?" Teresa stood over Jamie with her hands on her hips. She poked her full lips out, and batted her long, curly eyelashes.

Jamie sat up on the side of the bed, wincing like the sunlight was hurting her. Her eyes were swollen from crying. She dropped her head, looking at the floor to keep from having to look Teresa in her face.

"Look, I…I..I'm sorry. I know I've been acting kind of funny lately. It's kind of hard being around you knowing you still hang with Elaine. We were all best friends, once upon a time."

"Before she slept with your man." Teresa finished her thought.

Jamie took a deep breath.

"I wasn't going to say that. I was just going to say that things are no longer the same."

Teresa walked away from Jamie and sat on the antique trunk at the foot of her bed. She sighed, heavily.

Tamyra Walker

"Look, boo, I guess I'm sorry. But I can't dis Elaine because you don't want to be friends with her anymore." She tried to keep herself from sounding aggravated.

"I mean, she doesn't want me to be friends with you. You don't want me to be friends with her. Hell, I'm sick of being caught in the middle. I told her she was wrong for messing with your man. She was dead wrong. And you a good one because if I were you I would've beat her ass…"

"I don't feel like having this conversation." Jamie said barely above a whisper. She looked up, finally allowing her eyes to connect with Teresa's.

Teresa frowned her face as she looked her friend over.

"Oh, you look like hell."

"I know you do." Jamie responded, feigning a smile. "Oh, my God." She said placing both of her hands over her mouth and hopping across her bed. She ran to the bathroom, buried her head in the toilet bowl, and threw up everything she had eaten or drank in the past couple of days.

Teresa walked to the bathroom door.

"Dang, honey… did you just lay up in here and drink your sorrows away?"

Jamie rolled her eyes at Teresa and flushed the toilet. She brushed her teeth before coming out of the bathroom.

"No, it's nothing like that. I'm pregnant." She said before bursting into tears.

"Come again... what the fuck did you just say, bitch?"

"I said that I'm pregnant." Jamie walked past Teresa and sat on the edge of the bed. "And please don't refer to me as a bitch. I know you are just playing. But I don't get down like that, okay?"

"Well, I'm sorry, hun. But, ugh, I need details, boo. We both know you're not with Jamel because he's with Elaine now."

Jamie looked as if she was trying to fight the urge to vomit again. She looked at Teresa and pursed her lips.

"What do you mean, he's with Elaine? Just because he was screwing her..."

"Yes, honey, he is with her." Teresa interrupted. "You are waaaaay late. But anyway, you don't care about him because you're knocked up by someone else and I want to know who. Exactly when did you jump back on the horse...bih- Oops! I meant, girl." Teresa put both of her hands over her mouth the way a little girl would when she knew she had said something she shouldn't have said.

Jamie glared at Teresa, shaking her head.

"You are far too old to act the way you do. And I don't want to talk about it."

"Oh, I get it," Teresa said giggling. "You think I'll spill-the-beans to Elaine, and she in return will spill-the-beans to Jamel. Even though he was screwing your best friend, you don't want him to know that you are screwing somebody." She shook her head at Jamie. "You sure are loyal. Looks like you're not over him, honey. You got knocked up by a rebound guy."

Jamie jumped up again and flew back to the bathroom. The vomiting went on for about five minutes.

"I can't handle this. This morning sickness is crazy." She said laying her face on the cold tile floor and balling herself into the fetal position.

You want me to go get you a ginger-ale and some crackers? Cause all the puking is not attractive, honey. I mean, ew."

"I'll be ok, Teresa. Can you just leave, please… or if you are going to stay- shut the hell up, will you?"

"I love you, too." Teresa said sarcastically. She picked her purse up off Jamie's bed. "Come on honey. Let me help your knocked-up behind back to the bed.

Jamie slowly stood. She held onto Teresa as she guided her back to her room. She eased down on the king-size bed and returned her goose down pillow back over her face.

"I'm so freaking miserable, man. I want this to be over with already."

Teresa rolled her eyes, thinking, *You and your theatrical ass. I already know I won't be in the delivery room with you.* You won't be messing up my French manicure, *squeezing the hell out of my fingers.*

"Get you some rest, love." She said. "But I'm not going to let you lay up in this bed and sulk like your life is over. You don't have to tell me who you're boning, boo. You know me, I'll eventually find out."

She walked over to the door. Just as she was about to walk out she turned around and said, "My co-worker is going to an engagement party tonight. She invited me. Why don't you come with me? And no, Elaine is not going to be there..."

"Whatever, Teresa. I'll come with you if you promise to leave me alone, now."

"Toodles." Teresa said as she put her Michael Kors sunglasses on and walked out the door.

Jamie pulled the covers over her head and tried her best to fall asleep.

Chapter 7

Vincent walked out of Yancey's barbershop wearing a smile bigger than he had ever worn before. His perfectly shaped pearly white teeth glistened in the early afternoon sunlight as he made his way to run a few more errands. He had a long day ahead of him but didn't feel the stress of it all because he felt that his life couldn't have gotten any better now that he was living-it-up with his A-1 from day one.

Alese was his heart, had been ever since he first laid eyes on her in the club, dancing with her then boyfriend, Joel Lemons. He couldn't help watching her through the night, and when Marilyn, his overweight, self-absorbed, clingy date, who had always been jealous of Alese, got tired of him watching her she told him, "Damn, if you want her that bad that you got to stare at her ass while you are with me then you need to be with her. Why you here with me if you want that bitch?"

"You know her?" Vincent suddenly asked, shocked. He was oblivious to the fact that he was being disrespectful. But the fact that Marilyn knew her had piqued his interest and he looked her in the eyes for the first time that night since he'd laid eyes on Alese.

Marilyn didn't say anything. She glared at him with eyes as sharp as razors. But Vincent wasn't moved. He was past women trying to control him with their so-called mean glares. He waved his hand at her dismally, refocusing his attention on Alese.

Marilyn knew Alese well. They'd been friends at one point in time… that was until Alese started soaking up all the attention. Wherever they were, she always had to be the center of attention. If any boy showed the slightest interest in her, there Alese was, turning on her charm, flirting like she always did to take the focus off her. It was as if she didn't think Marilyn was worthy enough to have someone special and the only reason she was friends with her was because she had always been on the frumpy side and she knew she would get all the attention. So, when Alese finally transferred to another school in the tenth grade, Marilyn thought she was rid of her forever. But here she was, many years later, still the center of attention. Marilyn was certain that she had to recognize her, even though she'd put on a considerable amount of weight since the last time they'd seen each other. Her facial features hadn't changed at all.

"Fine, you bastard." Marilyn said, her voice dripping with anger and disappointment. She stood and turned around to face Vincent. "I'm leaving, asshole."

"Bye." Vincent said, catching a slight attitude.

Marilyn looked at him like her feelings were hurt. Her eyes welled up a little but then she realized that she didn't need to be crying over any man. She threw the single rose he had given her at him and without another word, stormed out of the VIP section and out the door. Vincent watched her leave. He hadn't meant to upset her. But soon he forgot all about her and his attention was directed back to that sexy woman he considered to be a goddess, on the dance floor.

An hour or so later, she made eye-contact with him while she slow danced with Joel. Vincent felt his heart would protrude out of his chest as he waved at her and winked his eye. She didn't wink back, wave, or smile. Her eyes looked dark and distant as she continued staring at him without blinking. Vincent's mental superman cape came out. He felt that he needed to rescue the poor little woman who probably was being starved of the sexual pleasure she deserved. He could see her spread eagle on his bed right then, doing things to her that would make her howl at him like a Coyote howling at the moon. One thing he knew was that his stroke game was on point. He caused many women to fall to their knees, begging and slinging snot, even offering to pay all his bills if he just stayed with them after he had put his almighty dick on them.

"The 'D', I've discovered, is a powerful thing. It causes women to be high as the sky when they are getting it, and go stark raving mad when they are not getting it." Vincent said to himself.

He made up in his mind that he was going to be Alese's knight in shining armor. He was going to rescue her and give her the love she didn't even know she was lacking. He kept close tabs on her through his best friends, Marlena and Donna, who always told him her every move. He knew about every argument she had with Joel. He knew about Joel's insecurity issues. Most importantly, he knew about his lackluster technique in the bedroom. He'd been having sex with Alese the way you would have sex with a nun if she was having sex, barely at all.

"That dude had the nerve to look at me like he was the man." Vincent had said to Marlena and Donna, shaking his head when he found out about his lack of ability to truly please Alese. "He need to be castrated if he doesn't know what to do with it." He said, knowing even more than ever that he had to have Alese for himself.

As soon as he caught Joel slipping, he made his move and placed his bid for her heart. He wasn't so sure what he wanted when he first met her. Really, he just wanted to know if she could twerk on him the way she was twerking on the dance floor.

Now more than ever, though, he was convinced that they were meant to be. It was high time for him to start acting like it. His grandmother, Beulah Mae Wiggins, a devout Christian and alcoholic, pretty much raised him and his sister. She had always told him that he should do right by a woman. His mother stayed on the run most of the time, and was too busy tending to her own selfish needs when she was around to pass on any kind of knowledge.

"Imagine how you would feel if a man was doing me dirty," His grandmother would say, in her heavy southern tongue. She stood, five feet two inches tall, was very thin, barely weighing one hundred pounds soaking wet. She sauntered over to the window to look at her flowers she had planted. The chrysanthemums were finally blooming and she couldn't help but to smile at their beauty as she wiped her greasy hands on her handmade apron that she'd made some forty years ago when she had worked as a seamstress.

"If you don't want the woman, let the child be. Cause son, I'll tell you this: when that bitch Karma get a hold to ya? Boy are you going to have a time, and not in a good way. These little piss-tailed gals ain't cut the same as they was back in my days."

She made eye contact with Vincent to see if he was listening. He was looking directly in her mouth, paying close attention to everything she said.

She smiled slightly and continued, "See, I have had my share of men. And they all was good to me. The ones I was married too and the ones that was dipping out on their wives." She paused a moment to note the expression on her grandson's face. He looked as if he didn't know whether he should feel embarrassed or surprised that his grandmother was admitting all of this to him.

"Now, I know what you thinking, Vincent." She said, half smiling as she put three more legs in the little brown paper bag that contained her flour and seasoning. She held the bag together and shook it.

"This how you make sure the chicken is seasoned just right, boy. But you don't know nothing about that... anyway..." She picked up the towel on the retro-styled table and wiped the sweat off her forehead. "It's too hot up in here for me to go to hell! Woo Lord."

Vincent smiled at the thought of what a character his grandmother truly was.

"I never told none of them men to leave they women at home, crying and whatnot. Hell, a few of em I ain't even know'd was married. I'm just telling you for your own good that you need to be good to your woman, boy. That ole saying, 'Hell hath no fury like a woman that has been scorned,' is the truth. I could tell you some thangs I done seen, starting with Sally Harrison, that woman across the way, putting roots on her man for beating her silly every chance he got and then cheating on her with her very own sister, dear Lord. Now, that's some Tom-foolery for you." She paused again.

"Aww, you ain't listening to me." She said, turning her back at last to Vincent. She went back to frying chicken, sipping whiskey out of her Atlanta Braves mug, and humming Muddy Waters, her favorite blues singer.

Vincent shook his head, laughing a little as he thought about that conversation he had with his grandmother all those years ago. Most of the time he ignored her advice. He was young, dumb, and full of cum, as his grandfather had always told him when he was out back with him cutting firewood for the heater during the cold winter months. But now that he had a woman on his arm worth having, he wished his grandmother was alive to see that he was making an effort to do what she had asked of him. And since he was doing such a fine job, he felt that God should reign down his blessings upon their union.

Vincent's downfall was and had always been that he loved women a little too much. The more he had, the merrier he was. Being a man who loved a woman's anatomy, especially those who had big breast and big butts, he knew he had a long way to go before he could get his little soldier to agree with him that Alese was the only woman he needed. But to further convince himself, he'd gotten rid all his side-chicks. There was only one left who just couldn't take a hint. Ms. Jamie Ferrell. He stopped allowing her to come over to his place. In fact, he had allowed his boo, to put her special touch on it. So, he had no choice but to get the hole in the wall fixed. He wanted to keep it as a memory of when he and Jamie was getting down and dirty. But if fixing it was what it took to make his lady, soon to be fiancé happy, then so be it. She was the queen. It was important for the queen to be pleased.

With pep in his step, Vincent walked to his truck, wearing a fruit of the loom t-shirt that showed just how firm his chest was. His biceps saluted everyone who dared to take a peek in his direction. A few of them whistled as he passed by them, perched like birds on their nest in front of the storefront barbershop that he'd been getting his hair cut at ever since he was eighteen-years-old.

Mr. Yancey, his potbelly barber, who dyed his beard an orange/rust looking color because he thought it was the trendy thing to do, had always done his cuts exactly the way he wanted him to. He saw no need to take a chance on anyone else. *Life is great.* He joyously thought as the sun cascaded down on his freshly bald head, making him look like a caramel version of Mr. Clean. The low haircut wasn't working for him anymore. He decided it was time for him to really step out of his comfort zone and go for the razor cut.

He stepped in his truck, turned the key in the ignition until it came alive, picked up his cellular phone, noticing he had a couple of missed calls from Jamie. A frown made its way to his face.

"Ugh, I wish she would leave me alone. Damn, I'm trying not to crush her, but she is about to leave me no choice. I got who I want." He hadn't told Jamie yet that it was over. He felt he didn't need to. His lack of communication with her should've been all the telling that she needed to get the hell on out of his life so he could be happy with his woman. An agonizing sigh escaped from between his lips as he ignored the little icon telling him he had a couple of voicemails. He pressed the number one on his phone. His face lit up with another smile when Alese face showed up on the screen.

'My girl is as smart as Einstein. I will give her that... and she is the most ambitious person I know. I wish some of those smarts would rub off on her when it comes to men, though. Now, I know I'm not the one to be giving advice, cause hell, I don't allow no man to get close enough to me for me to get burned anyway... but my boo need to get it together, and fast. These men don't deserve the energy she be giving to them. All they want is sex anyway... so maybe she just need to give them what they want and keep it moving. It's hard to trust anyone anyway with the money that she makes. She can be satisfied and still have all of her money in her account'

~Teresa Tipton~

"Well, don't you look cute." Teresa, Jamie's tight-eyed, skin the color of peanut butter friend, gave her a complete look over as she sashayed into her upscale stucco apartment building. She wore a black loose-fitting Chanel romper that came off her sleek shoulders. Her hips fanned out like the feathers on a peacock as she turned to disarm the alarm. The low cut romper showed off the massive tattoo of the cheetah she'd gotten inked on her left shoulder when she was only sixteen-years-old. Her hair was swept up into a chignon ponytail with bangs in the front, streaked with blonde highlights. Her high heeled black jimmy choo strappy pumps were tied around her long gazelle legs. They always made her look as if she had just stepped off the cover of a magazine.

"Obviously not as cute as you." Jamie responded as she eyed her best friend with envy. Teresa had always had the perfect shape, even though she pigged out just about every day like eating was going out of style. She turned around to look at her figure in the mirror, suddenly feeling a little insecure. "I can't be that far along." She said to herself, noticing the small bulge in her stomach. Unlike her friend, Teresa, who always loved to wear black, she decided to wear navy. Her navy sleeveless jumper made her skin look radiant as she made sure to put just a dab of blue eye shadow on her eyes as well. Jamie had just finished dowsing her skin with Nivea lotion before Teresa came barging into her home, without knocking, the way she always did. She was glad that she'd straightened her natural hair, and it hung almost midway her back. It was a huge difference from the puff she usually wore. The silver hair clip she wore on the front to keep her hair from falling in her face showed off her youthfulness. Her skin was flawless. She didn't have the first blemish that would obscure her beauty.

"We're going to be late." Jamie said, suddenly excited about the engagement party. It made her think of how happy she would be when Vincent finally popped the question. While waiting for Teresa to come back to get her, she had a lot of time to think about things. Vincent hadn't answered her call when she tried to call him earlier. But she figured he had to be busy at the gym since she knew he'd taken on a few more clients. She smiled to herself, thinking about just how sexy and lean he was, deciding right then she wasn't going to let her relationship with Vincent be water under the bridge. She was going to sit him down later tonight, after the party and get him to agree for them to start anew. Maybe they needed to take a sabbatical from all the sex they'd been having. She was already pregnant, anyway. Besides, sex had a way of sometimes misconstruing things. It didn't matter to her. All she wanted was her man. She put in work and felt if anyone deserved his heart it was her.

"Ugh, ma'am?" Teresa said, popping her lips. Jamie looked at her, slightly annoyed.

"Don't be looking at me like that. Your lil behind so deep in thought, you didn't even hear me calling you, not one time, bi…, oops, I meant, girl, but twice…" Teresa giggled lightheartedly, showing off her gold capped tooth. She called everybody, "bitch" whether she liked them or not. She couldn't believe Jamie was tripping about it all of a sudden. She assumed it must have been the pregnancy hormones.

"Will you just say what you're going to say?" Jamie fussed. "I'm so over you doing all of this extra stuff."

Teresa rolled her eyes and popped her lips again.

Tamyra Walker

"I know we're not rolling in this lil Camry I got. We bout to show up in that cute Infiniti you got sitting out there, girl. Must be nice to be a nurse… making the big bucks."

Jamie ignored Teresa as she set her alarm system and locked the front door. "Fine. We can drive my SUV." She mumbled, unlocking it with her keyless entry remote.

Teresa immediately began to do her so-called sexy walk. It was the walk she did whenever she was about to go to the club or anywhere where she was bound to meet a potential boo. She hopped in the front seat of the SUV and immediately opened the sun visor to make sure her plum lipstick wasn't smeared. She took her black J'adore framed glasses out of her purse and put them on.

"So, are you ready to tell me who been all up in you… and got you pregnant at that?" Teresa looked at Jamie and narrowed her eyes, like she was daring her to lie.

Jamie's eyebrows furrowed.

"I already told you, I don't want to talk about it." Her voice was stern.

"Fine Missy. I'll back off for now." Teresa pushed her glasses up on her face and started bobbing her head to Bob Marley's song *No woman, no cry.* Jamie had always been a fan of Bob Marley. She had every piece of music he'd ever sung stored in her cloud. His music made her feel serene when deep down within her soul she was bothered.

Jamie shook her head at Teresa, frustrated that she was insisting on keeping her keen nose in her business. *I'm not constantly asking her about that twenty-three-year-old boy she's screwing.* She thought. They rode the rest of the way in silence.

****

Donna walked through the side entrance of the Marriot hotel where her lifelong friend Vincent was about to celebrate his engagement with his longtime girlfriend, Alese. Over time she had grown to be somewhat happy for him, but at the same time she was kind of bitter. Even with having her own piece of man, Marcus, at home, it was getting hard for her to hide how she felt about Vincent. She'd always thought she would be his girl. She tried to show him in subtle ways that she was feeling him. Either he didn't want to notice her advances, or he was truly blind. Vincent had always regarded her as one of his homies and never paid her any attention. She'd gone out and bought the sexiest dress for prom, thinking that Vincent would ask her to be his date, but he chose to show up on the arm of LaDaisha Timmons, the one girl that Donna could not stand because Vincent treated her like she was royalty.

Tamyra Walker

Donna tried not to feel some type of way when they stole everybody's attention at the prom with their smooth dance moves. She simply exited out the back door, losing one of her glass slippers in the process. She went home, popped a couple of Mollies and called up Patrick Ingram to come and set her straight sexually.

Vincent didn't even look at her differently after she slipped the date rape drug, Rohypnol, in his drink at their high school graduation party. She was a couple of credits shy of being able to graduate. But that didn't mean that she was going to miss the party. She invited Vincent up to her hotel room that she got in her parent's name, using their ID and credit card. She had bought herself the most erotic negligee she could find at Victoria's secret, the kind that had the crotch less underwear.

When Vincent strolled up to her room at the very same Marriot he was about to have his engagement party, Donna was already wearing the negligee, sitting on the side of the bed, waiting for his arrival. He looked at her body like he was hungry and immediately begin to back up a little as if he sensed that he wasn't supposed to be there. But she knew that he wanted her, and she was hell bent on curbing his appetite. Vincent reached out his hand to touch her. Donna took his hand and rubbed it across the thin hairs outlining her vagina.

"Ssssssssss..." He said, as he snatched his hand back like he had touched something hot. Donna smiled seductively. "I'm all yours, boo." She said as she pushed him down on the bed. They tussled together on top of the striped comforter until he was naked. She looked down at what he had to offer, smiled weakly and straddled him. She eased herself down on him and moaned loudly as he was bigger than she anticipated.

"Wait. I need a condom." He said, reaching for his wallet on the bedside table. Donna took her forearm and knocked it on the floor. She leaned forward and placed her lips against his to make him be quiet.

"That feels good, doesn't it?" She asked, as she rode him like he was a saddle at the rodeo. Her voice was soft, making her seem to be the sweetest person in the world. Eventually, he stopped fighting the feeling, allowed himself to enjoy the ride. He swelled inside of her as she squeezed him with her insatiable walls. When he was about to cum, she held him down so that she could welcome all his love inside of her. It might've been wrong how she went about getting him, but once he discovered she was pregnant with his child he would have no choice but to love her. That was until six weeks later after conceiving, and two weeks after she heard the baby's heartbeat, Donna started cramping at work.

Tamyra Walker

The cramps were so severe that she was slumped over in her chair, sweating, barely able to compose herself. She went to the bathroom and discovered she was bleeding. Scared out of her mind, she fished her cellular phone out of her purse and called Marlena. But she was too busy, gallivanting with Milton Hughley, her latest fling, all over town to be there for her. To be honest she was kind of glad. She knew that she would have a lot of explaining to do. Marlena would never forgive her for not telling her that she was pregnant. And then afterwards, she would grill her nonstop about who the father was. Donna didn't want to have to lie to her. That would be like putting the nail in her own coffin. With tears streaming down her face she racked her brain trying to figure out who she could call. She couldn't exactly call her mother. Her mother would beat the baby out of her before she could run to safety. She swallowed hard, bit the bullet and finally called Vincent.

"Yeah, talk to me." He said answering the phone.

"Vincent, I need your help." Donna's voice was filled with panic.

Vincent sat up straight in his chair.

Aye, turn that radio down." He said to his homeboys Jerrod and Timothy. "What's wrong, Donna?" He asked, a hint of concern seasoning his deep voice.

"I…I'm bleeding… I think I might be having a miscarriage."

"Miscarriage? Come again?" He said, obviously shocked. "When the hell did you get pregnant and who are you pregnant for? Why that bitch won't come see about you?"

I wish I could tell you that you are the father, Vincent. God knows I want you to caress me with those nice thick lips right now. I want to feel you holding me... squeezing me, telling me that you'll die for me and our unborn child. Donna's thoughts were getting the best of her. Before she knew it, she was sobbing even more.

"Damn, girl. I'm sorry. I...I...shouldn't have said that to you. A...are you going to be okay?" Vincent shook his head at how careless he had been with his words. "What you need me to do, boo?"

"Can you take me to the hospital, please?" Donna's anxiety grew more as she felt more blood pouring out of her.

"I'll be right there." Vincent jumped out of the chair and ran for the door. "Aye, I'm out. I got to go take my friend to the emergency room." He said to his homeboys and at the same time disconnecting the call between himself and Donna.

Five hours later, Donna was heading back to her mother's house with tear streaked eyes. She stared out the window with her hand up to her chin as Vincent chauffeured her. All she wanted to do, after losing her baby was lay down, and tune the whole world out. Vincent pulled up in front of her parents manufactured home, and parked.

As she started to get out of his crown Victoria, he pulled her into his arms, holding her close. She allowed herself to sob in his arms. She only had a few hours to grieve. After this day she would never speak of it again. She would resume being Vincent's best friend, not his woman, and not the mother of his child. She would never tell him she miscarried his baby. She'd never tell him that when she raped him that she had purposely gotten pregnant. She knew that he didn't look at her the way she looked at him. So, she was going to let it go. But the pain of being in love with him for so long and not being able to have him had hurt her in a way she hadn't known was possible. Everybody thought she was heartless. But she had feelings. She was in love. The love just wasn't reciprocated.

"Damn, girl. That dress is tight." Marlena stood back, admiring her friend.

Donna rolled her eyes.

"I guess you look alright, too." She said brushing the sad feelings further out of her thoughts.

"If I didn't know any better, I'd think you was feeling some type of way about something…" Marlena said, looking at her inquisitively.

"Whatever." Donna said, waving her hand at Marlena and walking over to the refreshment table to get herself something to drink. She wanted the strongest thing available. She smiled brightly when she saw the bottle of Paul Masson Brandy. She was about to get tore up. The last thing she needed was Marlena trying to feel her out.

"What the world is that bitch doing here?!" Marlena asked, sounding a little shocked and aggravated at the same time.

"What, bitch?" Donna asked. She glanced at Marlena who was pointing in the direction of Jamie.

"Ohhhhhh! That bitch!" Donna said, laughing, totally forgetting how solemn she had just been. She snapped her fingers and did the cabbage patch as she thought about the drama about to go down.

"Shit just got real." She took a sip of her Paul Masson and walked over to meet Teresa who was walking side by side with Jamie.

"So, boo. I'm glad you came." She said, totally ignoring Jamie standing there with a stunned expression on her face.

"Yeah, and I brought my bestie with me." Teresa responded.

"I see." Donna said with a smirk. "It just so happens that I know her very well." She looked Jamie up and down and rolled her eyes. "Jamie." she said, acknowledging her at last. She looked off before Jamie had a chance to say anything.

This bitch is going to keep on screwing with me until I finally have to reach out and touch her stupid behind. I hope she doesn't think she

89

Tamyra Walker

is hurting me because she doesn't want to speak to me. I'm allergic to fake anyway. Jamie thought.

Jamie shook her head and grabbed a glass of water that the server was carrying on a tray. She didn't like having these kind of thoughts about anyone. However, enough was enough. Being nice was very becoming of her. She did it well. But sometimes, it was necessary to put a thot in her place. Donna and Marlena thought because Jamie was a career woman, she would hold her mouth closed like a virgin holding her legs closed and allow them to keep saying whatever they felt that they were big and bad enough to say to her. They were wrong. But she wasn't going to show out tonight. There was a time and place for everything. Tonight was a night to be classy. She knew that she would eventually have her chance to release all of her pent-up aggression. That was if they didn't catch her hands instead.

"Ah hem! May I have your attention." All eyes followed the voice standing up at the front of the room. Vincent stepped up to the podium looking dapper, to say the least, in his linen suit. Jamie had gone to a nurses retreat in Cozumel, Mexico with a few of her nurses a couple of months ago. She stopped at Bloomingdales in Miami, Florida on her way back and decided to surprise Vincent with the linen suit he was wearing at that very moment. She smiled weakly, suddenly not feeling so good. The alarm on her intuition was blaring loudly. She knew something dramatic was about to happen. She had a feeling that it wasn't going to be in her favor, either.

"We are all gathered here tonight to celebrate a very special event in my life."

What event could that be? Jamie wondered. *How come I didn't know about this event?* The moment that she saw Vincent, she forgot she was at an engagement party, as she was certain that Vincent was all hers.

"I couldn't be happier than to share with you all- the love of my life..." He looked behind him, reaching for Alese hand.

He then glanced out in the audience and spotted Jamie staring at him with her mouth dropped wide open.

"Oh, shit." He said into the microphone before dropping it on his chocolate Stacy Adams shoes- that Jamie had also bought.

"What's wrong, babe?" Alese asked, stepping up to the podium beside him. She was dressed in a lavender maxi dress with long slits up both sides and she wore micro braids. They were pinned up into a bun with decorative hair pins sticking out. Her purple eye shadow accented her outfit perfectly. She was beautiful. But Jamie had one problem with her, she was standing next to her man.

Tamyra Walker

Jamie rubbed her eyes, like they were deceiving her when Alese smiled at Vincent and kissed him on the cheek. She then linked her arm through his and laid her head over on his shoulder. Her beauty put Jamie in the mind of Halle Berry. She was slender like Halle Berry, too.

"Do you see this shit?" Donna asked gleefully, nudging Marlena in her side.

"I see this shit, boo." She responded. "This is too good." They both looked over at Jamie who stood there looking like she was about to pass out.

Teresa averted her eyes to Jamie as well.

"They look so cute together, don't they?" She asked her friend, noticing how all the color had drained from Jamie's face. "What the hell is wrong with you?" She asked, reaching out to touch her forehead. "You look like you have just seen a ghost. Is it the baby?"

"The baby?!" Donna, Marlena, and Vincent all said in unison before Jamie passed out in Teresa's arms. Donna looked at Jamie with her face balled up and bolted out of the conference room, trying hard to hide her tears. She had to pull herself together quickly or her cover would be blown. No one would understand why she left the room in tears when she was only supposed to be Vincent's best friend. She stood in the bathroom dabbing at her eyes. "How dare he get that bitch pregnant? But I lost our baby." She blew her nose, and with a shaky hand, reapplied her makeup, walked back to the conference room, and pretended all was well. That was the only option that she had. She knew that she would draw unnecessary attention to herself if she was gone for too long.

Tamyra Walker

Chapter 8

Teresa kneeled over Jamie, frantically shaking her and pouring cold water on her face. *A perfectly beat face gone to waste.* She thought in the back of her head.

"She's over here." She said, motioning for the paramedics when she saw them walk through the door with the stretcher. She felt a little faint herself. As much trash as she had talked she'd never in her life seen anyone just fall right smack out in front of her. She felt helpless, not knowing what to do to help her friend. She could take a lot of things. But feeling helpless was high on her pet peeve list. That and gum smacking would drive her crazy.

Donna and Marlena stood back giggling amongst themselves. They couldn't care less about Jamie fainting. Marlena was just being messy. But Donna was trying extra hard to pretend that she wasn't upset. Marlena pulled out her Samsung note, and posted a status update on Facebook: "When you chilling at your best friend's engagement party and his side bitch passes the fuck out when she sees that he has a beautiful wife to be. Lol. That whore actually thought she was number one."

Donna was the first one to hit the "like" button and commented: "Poor little tink tink. Hope that lil bastard in your belly die, bitch."

Vincent paced back and forth, nervously, while Alese looked at him, wondering just how much he had to do with the drama unfolding at their engagement party. He allowed his eyes to meet hers briefly, but quickly dropped them to the floor when he noticed that she was glowering. He knew that he wasn't going to be able to lie his way out of this situation. That made him pace even faster as he uttered a few unpleasant words under his breath. He didn't seem to be the least bit concerned about Jamie. All he wanted to do was save face with his fiancé. No one had ever broken up with him before. He was afraid that tonight would be the first time a woman gave him the boot.

"Her vital signs are stable." The paramedic with the long dreads and freshly shaven goatee spoke. "I think that she is going to be okay. We'll get her to the hospital so that they can check on the fetus." He looked over at Donna and noticed that she was staring at him.

"He is some kind of sexy." Marlena whispered in her ear.

"I know. Damn, right he is." Donna responded, as she continued undressing the young paramedic with her eyes. Slightly annoyed, Teresa nudged him on his shoulder. He quickly refocused his attention on Jamie.

"Now, I'm not the doctor, but I believe that your friend will be good as new in a day or two." Teresa breathed, a sigh of relief.

"Thank, God." She said barely above a whisper. She placed her hand in Jamie's hand.

"Hun, I'll be right behind the ambulance, okay?" She grabbed Jamie's purse and her keys and headed in the direction of her cream Infiniti QX80.

Jamie didn't say anything. Tears rolled down her cheeks as she was lifted into the ambulance. She was so embarrassed. She could have sworn that she saw a smirk on both Marlena and Donna's faces when the paramedic shut the doors to the ambulance. But they were the least of her worries right now. As she quickly scanned the audience of onlookers she had caught a glimpse of Vincent's face. He looked at her like he despised her. Jamie's lips quivered, as his hurtful glare made her feel even worse. She secretly wished that she would miscarry his baby. Suddenly, the fetus felt like an intrusion that she wanted to be rid of as soon as possible. If she didn't miscarry, she was going to schedule an abortion as soon as she was released from the hospital.

Not only had her baby's father deceived her, but he was *engaged*. The reality of why he'd been treating her differently over the past few months finally sunk in, and her blood pressure began to rise. *How dare he step to me on the subway that day, acting like he was consoling me when he had a woman of his own. I feel like such a damn fool. Why do I always do this to myself? I'm starting to feel like there is something wrong with me.* Jamie's thoughts taunted her. The tears began to flow more rapidly. A few seconds later the alarm on the portable blood pressure machine began to go crazy.

The dreadlocked paramedic looked at her. He felt sorry for her. "Ms., I don't mean to be in your business," He mumbled while readjusting the cuff on her arm. "But if it's a guy that's got you feeling this way, you have to know that he's not the one for you. A man who loves you would never see you hurting like this. He definitely wouldn't be the cause of the hurt. Now, I know it may take some time to get past the pain, but you should count your lucky stars that you are free. Now, you have the chance for real love to come your way."

Another tear slid down Jamie's face as she closed her eyes and tried to block out the painful thoughts of what had just transpired.

The twenty-minute transport to St. Martin's hospital was the longest twenty minutes of Jamie's life. She was so glad that she wasn't going to the hospital that she worked for. She was known by just about everyone there. There was no way that she would have been able to handle all the curious stares that she was bound to receive from her coworkers and subordinates that she saw just about every day.

Just a few hours earlier, Jamie cradled her growing baby bump in her full-length mirror. She smiled widely as she imagined the look of excitement that Vincent would give her when he knew that she was carrying his baby. She assumed he would walk up to her, kiss her lightly on the forehead, stoop down on one knee, kiss her belly and rub it, while talking soothingly to their baby. They would embrace and she would wipe away his tears of joy, just as he picked her up in his arms, carrying her to the bed to make sweet passionate love to her. She had already decided that if she had a boy his name was going to be Vincent Jr, after his father. And, if she had a girl, her name would be Victoria Malina. She had never seen Vincent's sister, Malina, before, but going by the way he talked about her, she was well aware that he loved her with all of his heart. He even had her name tattooed on his arm. So, she knew that he would be so proud for their daughter to have his sister's name.

Now, since things didn't go the way that she'd planned for them to go, all she wanted to do was ignore the baby that was moving around inside of her. Her syncope episode had obviously upset the fetus, but it was very much alive.

"Oh, this baby has a strong heart beat." The sonographer said to Jamie. She smiled as she pointed at the baby on the screen. "And, look-a-dere, there is the face, that's a sweet little face." She continued smiling. The fact that the sonographer was happy and she wasn't made her sick to the stomach.

"Awww, I think I might make your day today…"

Nooooooo! Jamie thought, as she pulled her arm over her face and cried silently.

The sonographer looked up.

"Are you all right, ma'am? Would you like to know the sex of this baby?"

"No." Jamie said. Her tone was daunting, as the sonographer looked at her, not knowing what else to say.

"Are you sure?" She asked.

"Yes. I am sure. What the hell you mean am I sure?" Jamie snapped. She sat up on the gurney and pushed the sonographer's hand off of her stomach. She swung her feet over to the side and stood. "Do you have a paper towel so I can wipe this shit off my stomach."

"Let me get that for you." The sonographer said, wiping the jelly off her stomach with a disposable sheet.

"If there is nothing else, I think I just want to go home. Do you have a problem with that?"

"Well," The sonographer said, totally stunned. "It is not left up to me, honey. The doctor is the one who decides when you are discharged." She stood and disconnected the machine. She hurriedly walked out of the room, refusing to look at Jamie again. Her attitude had definitely ruffled her the wrong way.

99

Tamyra Walker

Chapter 9

Five months later…

Jamie grimaced as Dr. Morrison checked her cervix. "You're ten centimeters dilated, honey." He murmured in his, Barry White voice. He walked over to where the nurse stood, dressed in surgical scrubs and a pair of boots, allowing her to help him get dressed in the sterile gown that he needed to wear to deliver Jamie's baby.

"Are you ready to have this baby?" He asked when he was standing before her again with a partial smile painted on his full lips. His moustache went up and down when he spoke as if it was a pair of raised eyebrows. Jamie felt slightly uncomfortable. He was standing right between her legs that she had positioned perfectly in the stirrups on the bed.

She could feel her heart beating fervently in her chest as she looked around the room, seeing everyone getting prepped for the arrival of her little one. She was downright terrified to meet the baby that she'd wanted to abort only a few months earlier. *Maybe the baby will know that I didn't want it because of its father.* She thought, weighted down with guilt. She still didn't know the sex of the baby. Even when she had gotten use to the idea of being a single mother, she hadn't wanted to know the sex. She wanted to be surprised when the nurse laid her baby on her.

"Don't push until I tell you to." Dr. Morrison said, glancing at Jamie compassionately. She didn't respond. Instead, she glanced at her new boyfriend, Michael Henderson, who was holding her hand. He pulled her soft hand up to his lip and kissed it gently and gave her a reassuring nod.

"You got this." He said, knowing that she was more nervous than she had ever been in her life.

Jamie and Michael had been together for four months. She'd met him one week after learning that Vincent was engaged. She'd scheduled her abortion at the local abortion clinic. But she'd had a change of heart when the abortionist had her to listen to the heartbeat. Her skin immediately became flushed. Tears gushed out of her eyes as she did what people called the 'Ugly cry'.

"I can't... I just can't... I...I can't do this." She had rambled on, hopping down off the table. She scrambled to put on her pants, leaving the clinic without even taking off her gown. "What kind of monster am I to want to kill a sweet innocent baby who didn't ask to be here?" She had questioned herself as she sped out of the parking lot, screeching onto the highway. She didn't know where she was going. But she was going to drive until her mind was clear.

Tamyra Walker

Two hours later she'd pulled into a Denny's, 120 miles south of her home. With all of the driving, she had finally noticed that she was hungry, and decided to have an omelet and some coffee. She was still riddled with guilt. Fragments of broken and distorted limbs had been flashing before her eyes, distracting her ability to drive safely. She had thought that feeding the baby that she was going to kill would soothe her fragile conscience. That was when she'd met Michael. He was sitting alone at the booth directly across from hers, dressed in a pair of khaki slacks and a buttoned-down collar shirt. His hair was cut low and his natural curls made him look boyish under the fluorescent lights. And he was what most girls would call pretty. His skin was light. He could have easily past for the actor, Mel Jackson's twin.

He hadn't noticed her at first, because his eyes were fastened to his newspaper. But when the waitress that they shared waited on her- he noticed her. Her skin was so beautiful to him. He placed a tip on the table, stood and walked over to her.

"Hi, my name is Michael. What's yours?"

Jamie looked up at him.

"I don't care what your name is. You're a man. That means you are a fuck nigga just like all of the other men. Because you have a penis, I'm sure that you don't know how to keep it out of strays. So, the hell with you and your name, you dog. And I'm not telling you what my name is. So, please just leave me alone."

Jamie surprised herself with her outburst. But at that moment, she didn't care too much about being civilized. She was upset and holding in any type of anger would make her sick. "What the hell are you all looking at?!" Jamie yelled at everyone in the restaurant who was staring at her as if she had lost her mind. Some of them whispered in hushed tones. "Y'all act like you've never seen someone act a fool before. Some of you do it all the time and twice on Sundays."

"Is everything, okay?" The waitress appeared back at Jamie's table with her eyebrows raised.

"I'M GOOD! I'M GOOD! OKAY?!" She put her hands up to her head and took several deep breaths. *You are losing it, girl.* She thought to herself. Slowly, she lifted her head and looked back at the waitress, sorry about her tone. "Can you get me some salsa for my omelet, please?"

The waitress nodded, and slowly walked away.

Jamie watched her until she was out of sight, took another deep breath and cut into her omelet. She was surprised when she noticed that Michael was still standing before her.

He smiled. "Now that you have gotten all of that out of your system, are you going to tell me what your name is?"

Jamie looked at him and shook her head.

"My outburst didn't scare you?" She asked.

Michael smiled again, showing off his perfectly shaped white teeth.

"Rarely anything scares me. Besides, I'm a man who wants what he wants. You are one beautiful sister and I must say that I want you."

Jamie rolled her eyes. *I never heard that line before. But I just know it's a line. Lines for men are like cell phones. They don't leave home without them.*

Regardless of her true thoughts regarding Michael, they went out a couple of weeks later and had been a couple ever since.

"It hurts." Jamie grunted. Her contractions were less than two minutes apart. She had been in labor for so long that her epidural had started to wear off. But being a nurse, and knowing the risks of having an epidural, she decided to bare the pain. She was thankful that she had been pain free for the past twelve hours and didn't want to complain now that she was experiencing some discomfort. Personally, she thought it was God punishing her for initially wanting to kill her baby.

"You're doing good, baby." Michael reached down and wiped sweat off her forehead. "I'm here, sweetheart. You're going to be fine." He whispered and kissed her gently on the lips.

Two hours later, Jamie welcomed her six-pound six-ounce baby girl, Amina Nevaeh Ferrell into the world. She cried as she looked her bright-eyed, extremely alert daughter in the face. She was the spitting image of her father, Vincent. But she had her mother's nose and mouth. She looked at her mother without blinking, sucking on her hand and wiggling her little toes out of the receiving blanket wrapped around her.

"Will you cut the umbilical cord for me?" Jamie asked Michael.

He looked at her, shocked and pointed at himself to be sure that she was talking to him.

Jamie nodded her head to reassure him. She had a half smile on her face.

"Sure, I will." He replied, proud that she asked him to share in such a special moment in her life.

"She's beautiful." Michael said, as he leaned over and kissed the baby on the forehead. "And you were a real trooper. I'm proud of you." His eyes glistened as he looked in Amina's face. "Our sweet little girl is here." He said, grinning widely.

Tamyra Walker

"Yes, Vin... ugh, Michael. She is here." *Lord, I know I didn't almost call him Vincent!* She silently thought as she gently rocked her daughter.

Michael pretended like he didn't hear the mistake that Jamie had almost made in calling him by another man's name.

"I'm going to go down to the cafeteria to get me a cup of coffee. You want anything, honey?" He asked as he walked to the door.

"No, sweetie I'm fine."

Michael disappeared up the hallway. Jamie stretched her eyes for a brief second, her mind totally blown that she was holding in her arms the sweet little girl she had just given birth to. She adored the baby for a few more minutes before her sister Janna walked through the door.

"My niece is so beautiful!" She said, walking over to the bed to get a better look. "Aww, look at my little sweetie." She cooed at Amina. Janna looked at Jamie and smiled. "Sis, you did good. Can I hold her?"

"Sure you can." Jamie carefully handed the baby over to her sister. She watched her with a big smile on her face as she did the most ridiculous baby talk ever.

"Tee Tee going to spoil that baby... yes her is... her shole is!"

The nurse walked in and smiled.

"We need to take her to the nursery now."

"Be careful with her." Janna demanded, as she handed her niece over to the nurse. The nurse smiled again.

"I most definitely will be careful with this precious little darling." She walked out the door with the baby in her arms.

"Well, sis. I hate to run. I have another class." Janna looked at her watch. "Shoot, I'm already late." She said while walking towards the door. "But that's okay. I just had to see my niece. I can't believe how beautiful she is… can't wait for mom to see her."

Jamie rolled her eyes at that comment. *She'll definitely try to find something wrong with her*. She thought to herself.

"I'll be back later, sis." Janna ran out of the door before Jamie could respond.

Jamie sighed heavily. "Well, I guess I better not put this off any longer." She picked up her cellular phone and called her daughter's biological father. He didn't answer. So, she left a brief message.

"Hey, Vincent, I just thought I'd let you know that our daughter was born a little while ago. She's so beautiful… the spitting image of you, with a few variations of me..." Michael walked back into the room just as she finished recording her message. He placed his piping hot coffee on the bedside table.

"Where's our baby girl?"

"Oh, the nurse had to take her to the nursery to get her cleaned up. They assured me they would bring her back as soon as I am moved out of labor and delivery."

"Good. I'm ready to hold my little angel."

Jamie looked at Michael with a concerned expression on her face. She had wondered for the last couple of months how he really felt about being with a woman who was pregnant with another man's child. Now that he was obviously showing that he was up for the task, she didn't know whether to feel spooked or happy. She decided only a few seconds later to be happy that she had a loving man who was by her side.

What was more surprising to Jamie is that Michael hadn't pressured her about having sex while she was pregnant. He was so understanding that Jamie almost wondered if he was having sex with someone else. She soon put that thought out of her head. *He's always around me. He can't be possibly sleeping with someone else... not unless he has a clone.*

****

Jamel walked onto the labor and delivery floor whistling a merry tune. He was going to be a father, finally and couldn't have been happier. Sure, he wished that he had chosen another candidate to carry his baby, but the fact that he was about to have his own child made him forget about how he wasn't so thrilled about the mother to be. Just a year ago he had said he never wanted to be a father. However, after his best friend, Malik, asked him to be his daughter's God-father, he was singing a different song.

Malik's baby girl, Cristalyn had worked her magic on him. He loved how she would wrap her tiny little finger around his thumb when he was giving her a bottle. His heart almost melted when she smiled at him for the very first time. His eyes glistened as he held the teething little girl in his arms.

Now, he was ready to walk down the road of fatherhood for himself. He had a few doubts how good of a mother Elaine would be. She constantly put her daughter, Shanna off on whomever she could get to watch her. And, she was *always* aggravated with the little girl. Especially when she asked her for something to eat and she didn't feel like getting up to make her anything.

****

"She's so sweet." Jamie said to the nurse, who was pushing her in the wheel chair, as she and her baby girl were about to be discharged. They were nearing the elevator, as she cooed lovingly at the little bundle resting in her arms. Jamel stopped whistling and turned on his heels when he heard her voice. He would know that voice anywhere. It was the voice of the woman he truly loved, but who had left him because of his infidelity. He thought about what a jerk he had been to Jamie when she caught him with her best friend's legs slung over his shoulder as she cheered for him to ram her harder. He regretted it almost to the point of tears. He hadn't had a home cooked meal since the last one that she had cooked for him. Even with Elaine already having a daughter, she hadn't the first clue about cooking. She thought popping a Michelina dinner in the microwave and pouring a package of sweetened kool-aid in a bottle of Dasani water was dinner. He wanted to apologize to Jamie for how he had treated her. But Elaine always discouraged him from doing so.

"What you want to apologize to her for? Her ass is the one who left you. Shit, my momma always told me that if your man found his way in another woman's bed then his woman must not have been satisfying him."

"Whore, you were in my bed." He said to Elaine and stormed out of the house, leaving her sitting there, stunned that he talked to her like that.

"Oh, so you want to be her little bitch, now?" Elaine yelled after him, bursting into tears once she realized how she had ruined things with her own fiancé, Eli, and now things weren't going so smoothly with Jamel, either. She could hardly deal with his snoring at night. He wanted too much from her. Jamie might have been a fool for him, but Elaine wasn't about to run his bath water for him. Ever. Not even if her life depended on it. She didn't run her own daughter's bath water. She figured that she had no business running his, either or massaging him. There were paid masseuse's who specialized in doing just that. He didn't even turn her on anymore the way he used, too. He always wanted to be inside of her, even when he came home from his management job at Waller's Pest control looking rough and smelling like bug spray. He didn't bother to buy her flower's on a weekly basis anymore. She couldn't understand why he was so hell bent on going out of his way to get her when he knew all along he wasn't going to continue doing what he did to get her.

Jamel watched Jamie like he was employed by the CIA and she was a criminal that they were profiling. *She's got a baby*. He thought, feeling a slight tinge of jealousy tugging at his heart. He cleared his throat and spoke.

"You're looking well, Jamie."

Jamie almost stopped breathing when she heard his voice. She hadn't seen or heard from Jamel since the day she left his home in a flash, with tears streaming down her face. She looked at him with an emotionless expression on her face. It bothered him that he couldn't

111

tell how she was feeling about him. Once upon a time, she would melt like butter if he walked into the room.

"I didn't know that you had a baby. I guess it wasn't so hard for you to get over me after all."

"Why are you here, Jamel?" Jamie finally acknowledged the man who had once been the love of her life. That was until he not only slept with her best friend, but showed her that he cared more about her friend having blood dripping down her forehead from where she clobbered her, than he did about breaking her heart. Now, she couldn't stand him. The sight of him standing there, having the nerve to be mad, made her want to puke. Not only was he a whore, but he also expected her to sit around sulking over him like when God crafted him, he was the only man He had made.

"My *wife* is in labor," he said, putting emphasis on the word, "Wife. I guess that is good enough reason for me to be here, huh?" He looked extra hard at Jamie's face to see if there would be any sign of pain.

Jamie didn't respond. But she felt the blow. She just wasn't going to give Jamel the satisfaction of seeing her hurt anymore.

"I...I'm married to Elaine, Jamie." He said, determined to make her feel some kind of way.

"Good for you." Jamie said, "Nurse, can we go now?" She took slow deep breaths to be sure her voice didn't crack. "There's nothing more I need to say to this man."

The nurse nodded, and rolled her to the elevator.

Oh, so she has the nerve to get that bitch ass nurse to roll her away from me while I'm talking to her? He angrily thought. *She's gotten awfully cocky.* He was expecting her to break down and cry instead.

"So, you were willing to get pregnant by the first nigga that gave your desperate ass some attention, huh?" Jamel yelled after her. "You were so worried about me screwing Elaine, but you got more miles on you than an eighteen-wheeler. I'm glad I cut ties when I did. You whore!"

Jamie swallowed the lump rising in her throat. She was not going to allow Jamel to get a rise out of her. She was a mother now, deciding she should conduct herself as such, instead of throwing low blows with a man she no longer considered important.

Tamyra Walker

Chapter 10

Four months later…

'After all this time, I finally got the woman I want. There is no way in hell I am going to let her slip through my fingers. I'm in this for the long haul. This girl is going to be mine until death do we part. I just hope that I don't have to be the one to cause the death. I've been trying extra hard to keep that anger thing people complain about under control'

~ Michael Henderson ~

~*~

Jamie walked through her apartment in a solemn mood. Today was Friday. Her daughter had just turned four-months-old. It was the first weekend Vincent was going to be keeping her. As much as she tried not to, she felt some kind of way about that. The last thing she wanted was for him to have some other broad around her baby girl. But there was nothing that she could do about that. She wasn't going to stand in the way of him visiting with his daughter. They'd just recently gotten past the anger he felt towards her for allowing another man to cut the umbilical cord when their baby girl was born.

"I can't believe you let another motherfucker get that close to my baby girl." He said, as he sat on the couch in her living room, holding Amina. Jamie walked out of the kitchen and handed him a bottle to feed her.

"Don't be mad at me. If you cared anything about having a daughter, you would have had your no good behind at the hospital." She threw a burp cloth at him. "Hell, I called you when I went in labor. You decided not to show up. So be mad at yourself."

"Just stop, Jamie. Okay. You knew exactly where I was."

"Whatever." Jamie said as she stormed in her bedroom and slammed the door. She didn't have any friendly words for him, and he'd tried hard to talk to her since she delivered his baby. He was leaving her emails, calling her all times of the night, leaving messages on her voicemail at work, and having a courier to deliver a dozen red roses to her every other week, which she disposed of immediately. She didn't want him. She didn't want his roses either- no matter how beautiful they were. She was finally able to deal a little with the hurt he'd inflicted. And she had someone else. There was no reason for her to raise suspicions with her new man, who was also helping her to take care of *their* daughter.

Vincent and Alese didn't get married after all. She left him after she found out he'd gotten another woman pregnant. To be certain she didn't have to have any more dealings with him, Alese asked to be stationed in Japan. Jamie had heard through the grapevine how Vincent was all down on his knees in Alese mother's yard, crying and begging her not to leave him.

Even though Jamie didn't have any words for Vincent, she had to admit that he was a decent father, although she was pretty sure that the reason he did as much as he did was because he was trying to win her back. She had no doubt in her mind that some of the outfits that he'd shown up with were outfits that he allowed other women to pay for.

Well, if the women he's dealing with want to be stupid, that is on them. She thought. *As long as he is doing his part, he can get it from the pope if he chooses to.*

"Screw you, Vincent… you and your wayward dick," Jamie said to herself as she stuffed clothes and diapers in Amina's baby bag.

Michael walked up behind her and placed his hands around her neck. He spun her around gently.

"Kiss me." He said, covering her soft plush lips with his. It seems as if he tried to suck the life out of her. She felt like a deflated balloon. He kissed her hard. It was as if he hadn't seen her in a long time and was making up for all the time he had missed. But he had seen her only a few hours earlier. He kissed her just as hard then and the time before then, five hours earlier.

"You've got to be the best kisser in the world." He said between kisses. He ripped the buttons on her blouse and buried his head in her breasts. "You so fine, baby. I can't help wanting you all the time." Jamie looked at him and smiled. *Why'd he put his hands around my neck.* She thought. She continued to look him in his big brown eyes. His facial expression was stern, as he reached down and smacked her a couple of times on her butt. Michael was five-years-older than she was. He definitely knew how to handle himself.

"I don't want you here all weekend long by yourself." He said, hoisting her up in the air and pushing her into the wall as he went for her lips again. "You're going to pack an overnight bag and come spend some time with me."

Jamie sighed heavily. "Maybe I can come tomorrow night, boo. I'm just going to…"

Michael tightened his grip just slightly around her neck. He covered her lips again, biting down a little too hard. He forcefully stuck his tongue in her mouth and pushed her harder up against the wall. With one hand, he yanked her dress up and found it in her silk underwear. He stuck one finger inside of her wetness first.

"You're tight." He said moving his lips to her neck and kissing her hard. Jamie moaned passionately. Michael placed all his weight against her and moved his lips down to her breast, biting her and sucking extra hard.

She wanted to tell him that he was pawing on her too roughly. The words just wouldn't come as he pushed her leg up and inserted another finger inside of her. He looked at her with an emotionless expression on his face. That made her feel a little uneasy.

When he was done fondling her he took his fingers out of her and licked her fluids off, never once taking his eyes off of her eyes.

"Your body reacts to me just the way it should." He said. "And, you taste so good. Pack your bag. You're spending the weekend with me."

Jamie looked at him, feeling a little more unnerved. She agreed her body had reacted to him. She liked how his fingers felt inside of her, but she didn't like the idea of him thinking he could tell her what to do. She liked him, but she was trying her best to take things slowly. She didn't feel as if her heart could take any more pain after what she had gone through with Jamel and Vincent. She started to object. He didn't give her a chance to say anything before he spoke again.

"I'm going to get us some take-out for dinner tonight." He picked up the keys to his truck and walked towards the front door. "Be ready when I get back."

Jamie plopped down on the edge of the bed as she heard the door close behind him. *Am I in over my head*? She thought as she took her fingers and massaged her aching temples. She felt in her heart that something just wasn't right with him.

Michael's attitude had changed to cheerful when she climbed in his big Hummer next to him. "I didn't know what you liked." He said. "I hope you like sesame chicken and shrimp fried rice."

"I like it just fine." Jamie relaxed against the big leather seat. She closed her eyes, exhaling slowly as, Will Downing's, *Wishing on a star* penetrated her soul.

"That's good." He leaned over and kissed her on the cheek before pulling out of her driveway. "And, I figured you would like Will Downing... his voice is so mellow."

Jamie nodded her head.

"It is."

Michael glanced over at her and smiled.

"I got baby girl a few things." He said after a couple of minutes of silence. "The bag is on the back seat. Check it out."

Jamie opened her eyes. She peeked in the back, grabbing the bag of goodies.

"Oh, this is so cute." She squealed with delight, smiling when she noticed the ruffles that had Amina's name monogrammed on the back of them.

"Yeah. Well, my niece, Elizabeth owns a boutique on 2nd Avenue. I don't go in there much. I must admit that I got her to pick these out for me. I wouldn't have known where to start. But from your reaction, I gather that she did a pretty amazing job."

Jamie didn't say anything. She smiled appreciatively rubbing her hand across the perfect stitch on the back of the ruffles. She was still feeling kind of bothered by Michael demanding that she come to spend the weekend with him. She could tell that he was trying to soften the mood. So, as upset as she was, she was going to put forth the effort to at least meet him half way.

"You know, Jamie," Michael spoke. She looked up to meet his eyes. There was a look of darkness catapulted in his irises.

"I feel like Amina is mine." He put his hand up, thinking Jamie was going to interrupt him. "Just here me out, babe. Okay?" Jamie nodded her head without saying anything.

"Now, sweetheart, I believe I was there with you when Amina was born for a reason. And, you letting me cut the umbilical cord..." He looked over at Jamie. He took his hand and raised her chin. "That was one of the best moments of my life. You and Amina belong to me.

I want to adopt her. And, I want you to be my wife. We can go shopping for a ring tomorrow, baby. I can get you any kind of ring you want. Doesn't matter how big, or how much it costs. I got the money in my account."

He turned on the interstate, reached over and grabbed Jamie's hand. "I can take better care of you and baby girl than that money grubbing piece of shit who broke your heart."

Jamie wrestled uncomfortably in her seat. No, she wasn't happy with how Vincent had treated her. At the same time, she wasn't the type of woman to sit and dog a man, regardless of what he had done, to another man. That in her opinion was plain ole foul.

Michael sensed her reluctance. He clutched her hand tighter. "I feel like the no good nigga lost the right to be in Amina's life when he wasn't honest with you. You got a real man now, babe. So, let me take care of you and our daughter. I promise you I'll do right by you two."

That unnerving feeling came back to the pit of Jamie's stomach. She'd always wanted a man to feel that she was worthy enough to be his wife and not just a live-in sex machine that he could turn on and off whenever he desired. But she wasn't feeling that enamored or ready to marry Michael. Slowly, her like for him was starting to diminish, as she was truly afraid of him.

"Michael, I appreciate you buying these things for Amina, but she has a father. You can be a part of her life because you are with me. But I'm not trying to replace her father. He did me wrong. Yes, he did… bu…but he is a great father to Amina." Jamie dropped her head, not knowing how Michael would react.

Suddenly, it seemed as if all the color had drained from his face. He snatched his hand out of Jamie's hand, focusing all his attention on the road. He didn't say anything else until they were sitting in front of his house in Emerald Falls. He pulled his truck into the garage and slammed on brakes. Jamie fell forward, hitting her head on the dashboard. The bag she held with the things Michael purchased for Amina fell off her lap onto the floor. As she leaned over to pick it up, she glanced at Michael nervously. He was staring straight ahead.

"Some weekend this is going to be." She mumbled under her breath as she unfastened her seatbelt and got out of the truck. They ate dinner in total silence. But every time she looked up from her plate, he was staring at her. Finally, he broke his silence.

"You're an ungrateful little bitch. Anybody ever told you that?"

Jamie stopped eating and looked at Michael.

"Why are you saying that?" She asked, pushing her plate away from her.

"I try to offer you something that you've never had before. I offered to make you my wife. I offered to adopt your daughter, make her mine, give your ass some stability- something you're obviously not used to. You should want your daughter to have a father so that she doesn't grow up being a little promiscuous spoiled brat like you, my dear, who thinks the world owes her something because of the mistakes that she made."

"Michael, I have had enough." Jamie yelled out. She pushed her chair away from the table and stood. "I'm getting my shit and taking my behind home."

"Wait, Jamie." Michael said as she stormed off. He walked over to her and touched her lightly on the shoulder. "Look, baby, I'm sorry. I didn't mean to yell at you like that... to, u.... ugh, treat you like that. I just want you all to myself. You are MY woman."

Jamie shrugged his hand off her shoulder.

"I agreed to come to spend the weekend with you after you pretty much demanded me to, didn't I? That should tell you something." She turned to look at him. "I am yours. But you need to chill out. You are freaking me out."

"I know baby... I know. I don't know what gets into me sometimes. I'm sorry. I promise baby. Can we please sit down and enjoy the rest of our meal, sweetheart?"

Jamie shrugged and reluctantly sat back down to the table. She didn't say anything else as she finished the last of her sesame chicken. Michael held his face in his hands, staring at her the whole time.

"Well, I guess I…I'll go and take a shower." She said once she drank the last of her wine.

Michael nodded, "You do that. I'll be up in a lil bit."

When he was alone, Michael thought about how beautiful Jamie was to him. He thought about how he had listened to her go on and on about how she never seems to find the right guy. He was trying to do right by her. But he felt that she was acting as if she had a lot of options when she would quickly open her legs for seemingly anybody who showed her a little attention. "Ungrateful, bitch." He snapped angrily, as he cleared the dining room table and prepared to retire upstairs.

A half hour later when she was sitting on the side of Michael's king-sized bed he entered the room and smiled at her sexily. Her shoulders once again began to relax. "Maybe he is finally unwinding." She said to herself. She finished oiling her skin, grabbed a magazine from his night table, turned over on her stomach, and began flipping through the pages.

"Get on your knees." She heard a gruff voice whispering in her ear. Michael grabbed her by the waist as he positioned himself behind her. He held her up and slid inside of her. He stroked her hard, grunting and biting her every chance he got. When he was about to cum he pulled out and released himself on her back. *She wants to be my fuck buddy for the rest of her miserable life, then I will treat her that way.* He thought as he flipped her over on her back and climbed on top of her, spreading her legs apart with his knees. He took one of her legs and put it on his shoulder. He inserted himself in her again and grabbed her around the neck while he beat the insides of her walls like he was mad at her. When he came the second time he laid on his back and told her to get on top. He plunged into her again, pulling her down on his manhood with all his strength. After ejaculating the third time, Jamie hopped off him and ran to the bathroom. He'd grinded her so hard that she was sore. She slid down in a corner and began to cry.

"This man is crazy." She whimpered as silently as she could.

Ten minutes later she tiptoed out of the bathroom and found Michael sleeping. She eased in the bed next to him and cried some more. A couple of hours later he woke up and straddled her face.

"Suck me." He said.

"Plea…Please, don't make me…" Jamie's eyes had just begun to get heavy and she couldn't believe that he was practically sitting on her face, trying to make her do something she truly felt was vile.

Tamyra Walker

"I said suck, bitch." Michael slapped her across the face. He forced himself in her mouth and began to grind hard, enjoying the gagging sounds she made.

"Yeah, you like that, don't you?" He asked, grabbing the back of her head and pushing her down even further. He wrapped her hair up in his fist and pulled so hard that her head flew back. "Don't you bite me. You hear me?" She nodded and he pushed her head back down on him. "You want to be my slut instead of my wife… well, how I feel in your mouth, slut?" He asked as he burst into laughter.

The next morning when he went to get out of bed, Jamie stuck her Glock up to the back of his head. She trembled and sobbed uncontrollably as she held the gun in place.

"I don't know what kind of sick, twisted, freak you are bitch- but I am leaving here, *now*. And, if you ever come near me again I will blow your demented brains out." She eased out the bed, crying still and backed out of his room with her hands still on the gun. He looked at her menacingly as she raced down the stairs. She picked her bag up off the chaise in his den and ran out the door. She was almost hyperventilating when she hopped in the backseat of the Uber that was waiting on her. As they were leaving Michael's house she looked up to note him standing in the door way. He hadn't even bothered to put on any underwear. He stood there, stroking himself, looking at her like he was going to have her for dinner.

"Get me the hell away from here." Jamie said to the UBER driver, as she glared back at Michael with her teeth clenched.

Tamyra Walker

Chapter 11

"Sissy, have I got the greatest news for you. I cannot wait to tell you. Call me when you get this message. This is far too good to leave on this answering machine. So, call me asap, okay?"

Jamie listened to her sister's delightful voice on her answering machine. Janna was a couple shades darker than Jamie, but she was also a couple sizes thicker, and exuded a carefree disposition the way that Jamie exuded being a sucker. Her wavy hair came almost to her shoulders and she allowed her hair to hang free against her milk chocolate skin most of the time. Janna's hips weren't as defined as Jamie's, but they ran neck and neck in the butt department. A couple of guys had teased Jamie when she was younger, telling her that's how they knew that Janna was her sister... they compared the butts and found that the circumference was identical.

Jamie still had a hard time accepting that Janna was all grown up. She was 22, about to graduate Summa cum laude with a degree in accounting, and unlike Jamie- Janna seemed to make better decisions when it came to matters of the heart. She safeguarded her heart at all costs. And she knew that not every Joe Blow was worthy of her time or affection.

"You say that now." Jamie said to her, almost thinking she was being a tad bit uppity. "But just wait until you fall in love, hun. You'll see. I promise you, little girl." Jamie waited patiently to get the calls from Janna in the midnight hour because she was heartbroken and needed someone to talk to. But it never happened, and after the third or fourth heartbreak, Jamie stopped calling Janna in the midnight hour to lay her heartaches in her lap.

"What kind of example am I being to let my little sister take on my battles? I have got to do better." She said to herself and vowed to do just that. That was until the next guy came along that she assumed would sweep her off her feet.

It was easy for Janna to say, "Leave that no good bum alone, big sis. Come on now. You can't cry your eyes out over every dusty nigga that you meet." But that was usually exactly what Jamie did. She believed in giving everyone a fair chance. Therefore, she found herself in a lot of unfavorable situations because of her beliefs. But despite all that Jamie had endured with her various boyfriends, she was proud of herself for the small progress that she was making. She had broken things off with Michael and that was something that she had never done before. She had always been the one to get dumped. Since the day that she stuck her Glock to the back of Michael's head, she had been free of him. She couldn't help feeling slightly better about everything that she had played a part in putting herself through. For once in her life, she wasn't interested in having a man under her. She was deeply wounded from all of the failed relationships that she had already been involved in and wanted some time to get herself together. She'd even hired herself a therapist to listen to her ramble on and on about her relationship woes.

Work was going better than she'd ever thought it could. Nothing made her feel better than going to work, caring for her patients the best she knew how, and then coming home and caring for her six-month-old daughter. Amina was teething and crawling all over the place, keeping her mommy busy. Jamie had to admit though, her little girl was the best thing that had ever happened to her. She was teaching her some valuable lessons that she'd never learned in any of her textbooks.

Jamie smiled as she picked Amina's blanket and toys up from the floor. Amina was on her knees, trying her best to pull up on the chair sitting at her mother's desk in her home office.

"Let me see what Janna wants." Jamie said, an edge of curiosity coloring her voice as she picked her cordless phone up from the base and dialed her sister's number.

"Well, it's good to see that you haven't forgotten about me." Janna said as she answered the call. "I thought for a second that I was going to have to put an amber alert out on you."

Jamie rolled her eyes.

"I could never forget your lil annoying butt, even if I wanted to. What you got so important to tell me?"

"Well, I just got off the phone with mom and I've decided that I will wait until this weekend when everyone is free to reveal the news. Mom decided to host a brunch to celebrate my good news."

"Oh, she did, huh?" Jamie couldn't help but to feel jealous about how it seemed as if their mother had always adored every little thing Janna did. Even with her having a Master's degree in nursing and maintaining a management position for four years now in a critical care unit, it seemed as if she could never do enough for her mother to be proud of her... not without her belittling whatever it was first. She remembered when she had first told her mom that she wanted to be a nurse. She looked at her and smirked. "You're just going to be a high dollar butt wiper. You would be making far more money if you were a doctor."

"Why you got to say it like that?" Janna asked. "You and mom stay into it about something. You just won't give her a break."

"Give her a break?" Jamie repeated, her voice elevated. She paused a second, erupting into her 'this shit ain't funny for real' laugh before she continued talking.

"You know what Janna? I wouldn't speak on things I didn't know anything about. Talk to you later, okay?"

131

Tamyra Walker

"Wait, Jamie…"

Before she could say anything else, Jamie hung the phone up in her face. *Her ass gets all of mom's love and affection and she has the gall to tell me that I don't give her a break. Hell, I'm the one who needs the break…*

Jamie stormed into her bedroom to check on Amina. She found that she had climbed over into the playpen, falling asleep next to her Mr. Potato head stuffed toy. Her facial features softened slightly as she witnessed her baby girl lying on her back, in her playpen, snoring lightly. She stood there watching her for a couple of minutes. "Poor little thing, wore herself out." She said before turning away to gather her bath salts for a long hot bath.

Just as she pulled a cozy pair of pajamas out of her drawer, she heard glass shattering a few feet away from her. She immediately fell to the floor, as she was certain it had to be a bullet ricocheting through the glass. She laid there feeling all over her body for the blood she expected to be spewing out of her. When she knew she hadn't been shot, she crawled over to Amina who had awaken from the loud ruckus and was wailing to the top of her lungs.

"It's okay, sweetie. Momma's here." She said as she held the screaming little girl in her arms, comforting her the best that she knew how. She sandwiched her body in between the playpen and her dresser, as she was too scared to walk over to her window. She was afraid that whoever was out there was still lurking around her apartment. Her eyes then averted to the huge rock that had landed on the floor at the foot of her bed.

"What in the world...?" She said as she glared at it, breathing heavily and massaging her baby's back. There was a note attached to it. She carefully scooted over to the rock. With shaking palms, she picked it up and read the note: **Are you ready to be my wife now, or do you still want to be my whore?**

"Oh, my God!" Jamie gasped, knowing right away that Michael had left her the note. She expected him to harass her the first couple of weeks after she'd left his house. She was relieved when he didn't. She assumed that he had gotten the memo, loud and clear when she had her gun placed firmly against his skull. Yet, here he was, almost two months later, bothering her when she was working hard to get her life on track. Jamie burst into uncontrollable tears. "Please just leave me alone." She said, as fear took control over her body. Amina began to cry louder. Her inconsolable wailing increased Jamie's tears as well.

The next day Jamie sat at her desk in her office at work. A migraine headache was underway the way that it usually was when she was completely stressed out. She had a hard time getting her baby to calm down after the unfortunate incident with Michael. She was upset too because she wanted to spend a relaxing evening at home with her daughter, catching up on, Grey's Anatomy, the only drama that she watched on television, and drinking a couple of glasses of the Merlot that she'd been given as a gift. Her plans were ruined. She didn't feel safe in her home, so she decided to pack herself and her baby an overnight bag, and went to the Hampton Inn on the other side of town.

As much as she had a right to be ruffled, yesterday's issues weren't doing her any good today. She had a lot to do, starting with approving the work schedule, as well as scheduling her nurses for their quarterly E-learning. She also had a couple interviews scheduled- one position for a staff nurse, and the other for a patient care tech. Then there were four or more nurses who were due for their TB skin test. And she still had a staff meeting with all of the other unit managers that she had to attend in the next few hours.

"How am I ever going to focus?" Jamie roughly pushed the stack of papers sitting on her desk on the floor. She could feel her stomach grumbling, as she hadn't been able to eat the Egg McMuffin she stopped at McDonald's to get on her way to work. "One thing is for damn sure. I'm not staying where I don't feel safe." She stood and walked over to her office door to make sure that it was locked. The last thing she wanted was one of her nurses to waltz into her office while she was handling business that didn't have anything to do with work. She didn't want to seem like a hypocrite, especially when she gave them the side eye if they had their personal cellular phones sitting anywhere on the nurse's station. She sat back down to her desk, propped her feet up, and turned on Ledisi's, *Pieces of me*, on her IPOD. Ledisi was her muse when she was feeling drained from life and needed a little inspiration.

As soon as she knew that the apartment complex was open, she phoned them. She had no intention of beating around the bush. She was going to let them know right away that she wanted out of her lease, effective immediately. "I'll gladly pay the early termination fee." She said to the leasing consultant, as her level of anxiety intensified. She then called a real estate agent. It was time for her to own her own home, far away from the apartment complex. Her daughter deserved her own back yard, where she could have an outside playhouse and swing set to keep herself busy when she was old enough. Jamie thought, *Michael will have no choice but to leave me alone if he doesn't know where I live.*

She felt better when the real estate agent, called her back within the hour, agreeing to go house hunting with her later that week.

"Now that I have that settled, I guess I will go to lunch." Jamie said, feeling excited about the great things happening in her near future. She sat at a table alone in the cafeteria, eating a Greek salad with fruit cocktail for dessert. When she returned to her office, bottled water in hand, she found a card on her desk. She figured it had to be a farewell card from her staff, as she had decided to resign her position as unit manager in a few months to take a position that would be available in PACU. The long hours that she worked were taking away from the time that she wanted to spend with her daughter. She didn't want Amina to ever feel like anything or anybody was more important than her. The last thing she wanted was for Amina to grow up and be a carbon copy of her... accepting hurt from any and everybody because she felt that was all she could fish out of life's sea. The thought made her have an even worst taste in her mouth about her own mother. Her mother had made sure that she had everything she needed materialistically. But Jamie wanted more than things for her daughter. She wanted her daughter to be certain of her love for her. Jamie felt that she would have been better off had she felt that her mother truly loved her.

"I don't feel like crying." Jamie said as she tore open the envelope she now held in the palm of her hand. You could literally hear the smile in her voice as she said those words. She opened the card and was shocked. It had two sentences printed in black ink: **Wife or whore, Jamie? Either way, you are mine.**

Jamie jumped to her feet. She ran out of the office and onto the unit. She held the envelope with the card in it high above her head. "Did any of you see who brought this to my office?" She tried hard not to feel spooked. But, she was literally shaking in her nurse mate work shoes as all of her staff stopped in their tracks to glare at the envelope that she had in her hand. They all shrugged their shoulders and went back to work. Jamie sighed heavily, tearing the card into tiny pieces as she once more hid herself behind the walls of her office. She had no choice but to pull herself together when one of her nurse's patient went into distress.

"How long has she been in V-tach?" Jamie asked the young, scared nurse as she walked into the tiny ICU room to assess the patient.

Tamyra Walker

Chapter 12

Vincent walked up to Jamie's door in the heat of the day, wearing his Nike work out gear with a Nike sun visor hat on his head. He hadn't called before he decided to show up. So he was surprised to see 'Hansel's and Sons' moving company, moving all of her belongings out of her apartment. Jamie had her back turned to him as he strolled up the sidewalk. She was bent over taping a box closed. She wore black leggings, an oversized t-shirt, and her pink and white air max Nikes. Her hair was pulled back in an afro puff that was in the center of her head. She also wore a pink Nike sun visor on her head. Vincent immediately felt a bulge in his pants. Jamie's butt was twice the size it used to be before she had given birth to his daughter. He could tell, too, that it was firm. He debated with himself if he should reach out and give it a little squeeze for old time sake. But Jamie wasn't feeling him that way anymore. He could handle her slapping the hell out of him for ogling and touching her assets. That probably would have turned him on just a tad. However, Jamie was still hurt over how he had dogged her. She would probably go over board and file sexual harassment charges against him just to be lowdown.

"I'm not going to take that chance." He said silently as he cleared his throat. "Soooo, Ms. Jamie Ferrell." He mumbled, alerting her that he was there. "When were you going to tell me that you are moving?"

Jamie stood up straight. She turned around to face Vincent, with a frown on her face. His Ralph Lauren aftershave hit her nose, causing her to throb just a little in the lower part of her body. *Damn, why is he doing this to me.* She was mad at herself for feeling that way and decided to lash out at Vincent.

"Hello." She said, being overly dramatic with her hand gestures. "My phone still works, you know. And I don't remember getting a call from you telling me that you were going to be at my place at…" She looked at her watch to see what time it was. "11:15. Yet, you are standing here in my living room like you have a right to be. Besides, I don't owe your ass an explanation. I'm grown."

Vincent rolled his eyes upward and shook his head. "Come on now, Jamie." He pleaded. "How long are you going to hate me? I am the father of your daughter. I don't mean no harm. I was just stopping by to see how my little angel was doing."

Jamie stared at him with a 'child, please' expression on her face. "In that case, you could have called the daycare, Vincent." She wasn't about to let him feel like he could soften her in any kind of way. She wanted him to feel pain for his actions for… well, forever.

139

Tamyra Walker

"It is a weekday, you know. And, it's not five p.m. yet. Call them up, or better yet, drop by. I'm sure they won't have a problem with you doing so." She glared at him for a few more seconds before turning her back to him again.

Damn he is still sexy to me. Oh, man I just had a visual of him pounding me from behind. Help me Jesus. Lord, I am weak. I'm weak, Lord. I'm weak! I'm weak! Jamie struggled hard to keep the tears of desire from falling down her face. If it wasn't such a shame, she would have told the moving company to take a long lunch break. She would have waited for Vincent to come back into the apartment, and she would have met him upstairs with the whip cream and honey they experimented with a few times before when she'd thought all was well.

Vincent wanted to be upset with Jamie for talking to him roughly, even though he knew she was just giving him a hard time. He played it off though, like his feelings weren't hurt. After all, he knew he had done her pretty dirty. He knew if it had been the other way around his attitude would have been ten times more foul. More than likely he wouldn't have considered forgiving her at all.

"Let me help you with those boxes." Vincent watched Jamie walk down the stairs to load a few things into her SUV. She didn't feel like arguing with him. Truthfully speaking, she didn't want him to leave anyway.

"Fine, Vincent," she said throwing her hands up. "Can you please not break anything? A couple of these things I got from abroad."

"Yes, ma'am." He said backing away from her, pretending like he was scared. It was his attempt at lightening the mood and perhaps forcing a glimmer of a smile out of Jamie. He knew that she was mad with him. But that wasn't going to stop him from trying to stick his penis in her panties. He hadn't felt her in over a year and could hardly control himself. When she placed her boxes in the trunk, she felt Vincent's manhood, swelling in his pants against her butt.

"Back up, now, Vincent." She said, taking a deep breath, "before I punch you, okay?" She shot him daggers that would have intimidated the ordinary guy. But he felt himself get just a little bit harder. *Yeah she wants it.*

"Oh, my bad." He said as if he didn't know what he was doing. He smiled devilishly as she walked back up the side walk, leading to her apartment.

Tamyra Walker

'I've been posing as his best friend long before I felt fire in my coochie for him. And now that Jamie is out of the picture, he is going to be mine at last'

~ Marlena Evans~

~*~

Marlena walked up to Vincent's door, wearing a pair of pink booty shorts, and a white tube top. She stretched out her long finger nails, colored in pink nail polish with white polka dots to knock on the door. "Wonder where he at?" She said, peeping through his blinds. Her heart almost stopped when she saw Jamie sitting on the couch. He had his arm draped across the back of the couch. Amina was sitting in the middle of both of them, playing with a soft paged story book.

"Oh, so he thinks he is just going to get back with that bitch, huh?" She said. She was so angry that she could hardly breathe. She took her fists and began to beat on the door really hard. She screamed his name like she was in imminent danger. The longer he took to come to the door, the louder the knocks became.

"What the hell is your problem?" Vincent asked, yelling through the door. He opened it with his pistol in his hands.

"What you got a gun for?" Marlena asked with her arms folded across her chest. Her voice trembled just slightly as she tried to gain composure of her labored breathing. Her chest was heaving like she'd been running in a marathon.

"Oh, it's you." Vincent said, nonchalantly. He breathed a sigh of relief, expelling a lighthearted laugh from his windpipe. "Why are you knocking on my door like that? Don't nobody knock like that but five O or some bitch that I don't want to be bothered with. You were about to get the business... real talk."

"So, I'm a bitch now? Is that what you're calling me?" Marlena retorted. She ignored everything else he said, deciding to focus on what she assumed to be the negative.

Vincent looked at her like she was crazy. He stuck out his hand to feel her forehead.

"I'm just making sure you alright, boo." He said. "Because you are tripping big time. What's up?"

"I want to come in, Vincent." She tapped her foot impatiently with her arms folded across her chest. She wore a dissatisfied glower on her face. "We were supposed to be talking about something, remember?"

Vincent rubbed his finger across his chin like he did when he was thinking.

"Oh, yeah, my bad." He said. "It's not that important. I'll call you later, okay."

"So, I can't come in?" Marlena asked, standing her ground. She was as stubborn as a bull and refused to move.

Vincent felt himself becoming irritated.

"Marlena, I'm going to need you to come back later, okay? I got my little girl in here…"

"And her whore of a mother, too." Marlena yelled loud enough for Jamie to hear her.

"Good bye, Marlena." Vincent said to her and gently closed the door in her face. Marlena began to beat on the door again.

"I'm your best friend, nigga! And I done seen that lil bih… girl before anyway. You don't even know if she is yours. You know that broad was trying to trap you."

Vincent yanked the door back open, his face contorted with anger.

"Marlena, have you lost your mind, talking about my little girl like that? What the hell is wrong with you?"

Jamie had already gotten up off the couch and put on her shoes. Over the past couple-of-weeks, she'd had a few conversations with Vincent that wasn't exactly all to do with their daughter. She regretted it now, because obviously Marlena was feeling some type of way for a reason. She knew in her heart that Donna had a thing for Vincent. She didn't know Marlena was feeling him, too. "It's none of my damn business, though." She said with an attitude as she packed Amina's bag. "He is not my man. I'm just his baby momma." She walked past Vincent, standing at the door with her daughter fastened on her hip.

"You don't have to leave, Jamie... Marlena was just getting ready to go." Vincent sounded desperate as he watched Jamie strap their daughter in her car seat.

"It's okay. I have a few more things to pack and an even busier day tomorrow, Vincent." She said as she walked around to the driver side and got in. She drove off without saying anything else. Her cellular phone rang an hour later. She didn't even bother to answer it. She already knew it was Vincent. She wasn't going to allow her life to fall back into shambles dealing with him. As far as she was concerned, Donna, Marlena, Alese, and anyone else who wanted him could have him, since he seemed to be for the community anyway.

Chapter 13

'There's nothing in the world I like more than spending time with my sister. I look up to her. Sometimes, I think I even idolize her. She means everything to me. She is not only a sister but my friend as well. I only wish she and mom got along better. Then our family would be perfect'

~ Janna Marshall~

~*~

Janna and Jamie sat together at the EGG and I having breakfast. "I'm sorry, Jamie. I was wrong to lash out at you the way that I did the other day. But I think this brunch tomorrow at moms couldn't have come at a better time. You two, really need to talk about things."

Jamie rolled her eyes.

"Apology accepted, Janna."

"So, how has my sweet baby love, Amina been doing, with her lil fat self?"

"Don't be calling my baby fat." Jamie said jokingly. "She is good. Spoiled rotten is an understatement. But I honestly wouldn't have it any other way, sis."

"Well, that's good. And what about her father?"

Jamie looked up.

"Now you're just trying to be nosy." She said in a reserved tone of voice. She picked her orange juice up and took a tiny sip."

"Well." Janna said, trying hard to justify her question. "When it comes to my niece, I have a right to be nosy."

"No, ma'am you don't." Jamie looked at her sister like she couldn't believe she was trying her like that. "You have a right to know how your niece is doing, but Vincent has nothing to do with this conversation. Now, I don't feel like going back and forth with you, okay? So, let's just leave it at that."

"Whatever." Janna remarked, feeling slighted. "You don't have to be so snooty about it."

"AND," Jamie said with emphasis, "you don't have to be all in my business either." She glared at her sister with a straight face. They both stared at each other for a couple of minutes. A commotion rang out in the restaurant and the stare down was aborted.

"What was that?" Janna asked. They both turned when they heard the commotion at the back of the restaurant.

"I'm just saying, Jamel. You could keep your behind at home sometimes. Elissa is your daughter, too. You need to be helping me with her, instead of running the streets with your homies all the time like you are still in your twenties. Your ass is damn near forty." Elaine was angry as she yanked a chair away from the table in the back of the restaurant and sat down.

"Isn't that your friend?" Janna whispered to Jamie.

"Hell, no that bitch ain't no friend of mine." Jamie glared at Elaine and Jamel coldly. She wanted to walk up to Elaine and savagely beat her. But neither one of them had noticed that she was in the restaurant. A small part of Jamie wanted to keep it that way. She didn't get to hang out with her sister much, and this was their day to simply chill and enjoy each other. Their next stop was going to be at the spa.

"Well, I know he used to be your boo." Janna said, pointing at Jamel.

"You said the key word, sis... he *used* to be..." Jamie replied. "Shhhhhh, I'm trying to hear what they are talking about."

Janna rolled her eyes at her sister.

"Look who is being nosy now." She took a couple bites of her ranch potatoes.

"No, I'm not." Jamie said with a shrug. She cut into her eggs benedict. "If they want to yell their business out in public, then they must want people to know about it." She turned around to notice that

Elaine was staring at her. They held each other's gaze momentarily before Jamel butted in.

"What are you looking at?" He asked her. He held the menu tightly in his hand as he turned around in his chair to see for himself.

He was frozen at the sight of Jamie's beautiful eyes piercing him like a dagger through a block of ice.

He stared at her for a few seemingly never-ending seconds before he spoke.

"What are you doing here?!" He asked, embarrassed that she obviously had heard how Elaine was yelling at him. But Elaine was frustrated, and having a new baby was overwhelming, especially since Elissa was often colicky and cried a lot. To make matters worse, her older daughter, Shanna wasn't doing a good job of accepting she had a baby sister. She still wanted to be the baby and often refused to acknowledge Elissa. She'd even been caught a couple of times sucking the baby bottle and deliberately wetting herself when she knew how to go to the bathroom.

Jamie looked at Jamel a couple more seconds before she shifted her eyes back to Elaine. She could sense the enormous amount of stress plaguing her world. But she didn't feel an ounce of sympathy for her. Besides, Elaine didn't regret sleeping with her man. She still

149

wanted to rub her nose in it. She had her hand held down that moment, so that Jamie could see her two-carat wedding band on her finger.

Jamie wiped her mouth, drank the last of her orange juice and stood.

"Well, well, well." She said, with a smirk. "Looks like everything isn't so beautiful in paradise." She shook her head at Jamel. "Tsk, Tsk, Tsk, you should've known better… a cubic zirconia could never be a diamond." She walked off without saying anything else.

The arguing commenced between Jamel and Elaine, as Jamie and her sister, Janna walked out the door. Elaine was now yipping like a restrained puppy because she felt that her husband had disrespected her by staring at his ex the way that he did right in her face. "I don't know what I ever saw in you!" She yelled.

"That's the same thing I wonder about you." He shot back.

Chapter 14

"Oh, look at my beautiful glam baby!" Leanne Marshall, Jamie's mother, reached for the highly energized little girl as Jamie waltzed into her house at ten a.m. on a Saturday morning. Jamie forced a smile and allowed her mother to take Amina out of her arms. She really didn't want to be there. But her sister, Janna, meant everything to her. She didn't want to disappoint her.

"Dear, Lord Jamie." Her mother said, grimacing. "What are you feeding this poor child? Why, she's as heavy as an ox."

"Oh, so you have held an ox before, mom?" Jamie asked sarcastically.

Janna sucked her teeth. *Please let this day go smoothly.* She was not so sure how things would transpire. She had to admit that her mother didn't have to say what she'd said to Jamie. For once she could see that it appeared as if she was trying to start some drama with her.

Leanne flipped her long-permed hair behind her shoulder.

"I would expect you to be flip at the mouth, Jamie." She said, sitting on the Queen Anne couch and placing Amina in her lap. "You know well what I meant."

"It's not my place to know anything. I took it exactly how you said it, mother."

"All I'm saying is, honey, you don't want her to be overweight like..."

"Mother, did you forget that I am a nurse? I know perfectly well how to care for my daughter." Jamie walked off to go to the bathroom. "Yes, I was chunky as a little girl, but so were you, mother, or did you forget? And even into your adulthood. Liposuction worked wonders for you, I'd say."

Leanne shot Jamie a cold glare. A gasp slipped from between her perfectly painted red lips. Janna stood with her hand over face shaking her head from side to side.

"Ah hem." Bill Marshall, Janna's father, and Leanne's husband entered the den, still wearing his plaid pajamas Jamie and Janna had gotten for him as a Christmas gift when Jamie was in her first year of high school. Janna was still in elementary school.

"I know that you ladies aren't getting into it already?" He shook his head, knowing that they were doing just that. But he wanted to diffuse the situation, if he could before it got out of hand. He gazed at his wife with a, 'can't you be nice?' expression etched on his face.

Leanne gave her tall and handsome husband a blank stare in response. He was easy on the eyes. Although he was approaching sixty, he barely looked fifty. He was in perfect shape. In fact, he still went on a sprint every morning except Sunday. His rippled chest made itself known, even though he wore a Celtics T-shirt with his flannel pajama bottoms.

Jamie had to fight a few of her friends in high school off with a stick. They flirted openly with him whenever he showed up at any school function. Some of their mothers were just as bad. Bill did mechanical work in his spare time, when he wasn't busy being an accountant. Often times, they pretended like their cars had serious issues, just so they could come to his shop. Jamie knew that he had to be a serious playboy in his days of youth.

Janna rose to her feet. "Dad." She said as she ran into his arms, squeezing him tightly.

Jamie froze where she stood, smiling brightly. Bill wasn't her biological father. But ever since he'd married her mother when Janna was only two-years-old, he'd treated her like she was his daughter. She admired him, secretly envied her baby sister for having a loving father when she didn't have one. Bill had always been like Mighty Mouse, saving the day when it came to his little girl. Jamie wanted that for herself from her very own biological father.

Tamyra Walker

"Come on over here, girl and give your pop a hug." Bill said to Jamie with his arms outstretched.

"It's so good to see you, dad." Jamie said as she fell into his arms.

"I was just about to say!" He said jokingly. "Don't make an old man pull out his belt on you." They both laughed together, as Jamie squeezed him with all her might. She looked up to see her mother scowling at her. She looked off when she saw that Jamie saw the expression on her face.

A loud knock on the door caused everyone to look at the front door simultaneously.

"Oh, that's Pernell!" Janna squealed with excitement. She ran to open the door. "You're early." She said, closing the door behind him. He grabbed her, lifting her off the floor as they hugged. "My parents are standing right around the corner." She said shyly as he lowered his lips to hers, kissing her with desire burning in his loins.

"I missed you, sweetheart." He whispered in her ear. Janna smiled. She reached up, running her fingers through his hair, kissing him lightly on the lips. He loosened his grip.

"Come on in the living room." She said, grabbing his hand, and leading the way.

"Mom, dad, you have met Pernell before. I asked him to join us."

"Oh, baby, that's fine." Her mother said, leaning forward on the couch to shake Pernell's hand. "Welcome to our home, young man. You two are so cute together."

She shot Jamie another menacing glare. Amina crawled out of her grandmother's lap and sat down on the floor.

"Put some cartoons on for that baby." Jamie's mother demanded. She stood and walked to the kitchen. Jamie rolled her eyes as she picked up the remote control to try and find a program that might grab her baby's attention.

Janna pinched her on the shoulder, leaning over to whisper in her ear. "Come with me, now." Jamie followed her baby sister down the hall into the study, that use to be her bedroom. She sat down in the office chair at the roll top desk. A smile erupted across her lips when she looked across the room and saw the old-fashioned singer sewing machine that had been passed down for several generations. Her mother was now the recipient and was supposed to continue the tradition by passing the family heirloom down to her.

"The tension is thick up in here. I could cut it with a knife." Janna said with a sigh.

"Tell me about it." Jamie responded. "Can you please hurry up and tell us what you got to say so I can leave here?"

"I don't know what mom's problem is." Janna said, her eyes filled with sympathy as she looked at her sister. 'That ox comment she made was totally out of line."

Jamie waved her hand dismally.

"I'm not worried about that. It wouldn't be mom if she didn't find some kind of way to put me down. You know that's her M.O."

"Well, I just wanted to apologize for her behavior."

"What the hell are you apologizing for?" Jamie snapped. She walked over to Janna, standing before her with her hands on her hips. "You don't have to apologize for her. Mom is grown and is responsible for her own actions… not you."

"You're right. I…I am sorry…"

"Will you please stop apologizing, damn." Jamie broke into an infectious laugh as she witnessed Janna's uncomfortable stance. She didn't know at that point what she should say.

"Now come on. I'm eager to see what's so important that we all had to be gathered together."

Janna leaned over and hugged her sister.

"I love you." She said as she reached for her hand. They walked back up the hall hand in hand.

"I was wondering where you two had disappeared to." Their mother said when she saw them enter the kitchen. Jamie and Janna gave each other a knowing glance, as they sat down in their respective seats. "You know we can't keep these fine men waiting too long. Let's feed them before they start acting up."

Pernell leaned over and squeezed Janna's hand. He admired her mother's wit. Leanne went about the kitchen, sitting all kinds of assorted bagels, Danish, and fruit on the table. There were also two pitchers of freshly squeezed orange juice, milk, and gourmet coffee.

"Now, none of you have to eat grits if you don't want to." She said, walking over to the stove and stirring the pot of grits. "But breakfast, brunch, or whatever, wouldn't be the same for me without my daily grits.

After fixing herself a helping of the piping hot grits, she sat down next to her husband and nodded her head. He knew that meant for him to say the grace.

"Let us bow our heads and pray." Bill said, motioning for everyone to grab hands.

"Amen." Everyone said in unison when he was done praying. All to be heard for several long minutes was forks and spoons clanking against plates. The homemade Danish and bagels Jamie and Janna's mother made were beyond delicious to everybody. Pernell took Leanne up on her offer and accepted some of the grits.

"These are the best grits that I have ever had! No lie." He said offering her praise. "Thanks so much for your hospitality."

"Oh, you're quite welcome, son." Leanne replied grinning. "And you are welcomed to join us anytime you please."

Janna grabbed a second bagel before clearing her throat.

"I don't want to make any of you wait any longer." She looked over at Pernell and smiled. He smiled back and winked. "I just wanted all of you to know that, my boo proposed to me. We are getting married next year on the beach in Maui, Hawaii."

"Oh, baby, that is such great news!" Her mother said as she stood and walked around to Janna's side of the table. "Come here, honey. Give me a hug. I am so happy for you… but most of all I am proud of you baby girl."

Jamie looked up from eating.

"That's great news, Janna. I'm really happy for you."

Their mother held Janna at arm's length.

"So, where is your man Jamie?" She asked, glaring at her with contempt over her glasses. I hope to God whoever you got this child by is the one you're still dealing with. I would hate for you to be bed hopping." Everyone in the room gasped.

Jamie put her fork down. She glared at her mother, unable to hide the hurt she felt. "Like you, mother? Is that what you are afraid of? You don't want me to be a sad ass bed hopper like you?" Jamie pushed her chair back and stood. She ran to the living room and grabbed Amina's bag, stuffing her toys in it before grabbing Amina out of the high chair that had been hers when she was a baby.

"I'm really happy for you, sis." She said with tears rolling down her cheeks. She peered at her mother one last time. She stood there with her hands on her hips, an evil smile etched upon her lips. Jamie opened the screen door and walked out. She sped out the drive way, leaving a trail of dust behind her. She pulled into the Winn-Dixie parking lot around the corner from her mother's house and sobbed bitterly while Amina cooed in the backseat.

Chapter 15

Two days later…

Jamie sat in the middle of her bed, in her new two story house. She held a glass of scotch in her hand, bathing in self-pity. That's all she had done for the past couple of days. She took an immediate leave of absence from work. The only reason that she had gotten out of the bed was to take her daughter to daycare. The one thing that she wasn't going to allow her daughter to see was her feeling sorry for herself and drinking her sorrows away. She looked up to see the light on her answering machine flashing. She had over twenty-five missed calls, and over half of the voicemails were from her sister.

Janna didn't have anything to do with how her mother had treated her, but that wasn't the reason that Jamie wasn't too particular about talking to her. She was green with envy because her sister at nearly twenty-three years old had already found the love of her life. She would be thirty in a few months and didn't have anything to show for all of her adult years except heartache after heartache.

"That bitch has a lot of nerve." She said, in reference to her mother. Her mother didn't know that she knew, but Jamie was well aware of her past life, how she used to be even before she had gotten involved with Jamie's father who she allowed to dog her. But she shouldn't have expected anymore from Levi, especially when she stole him from Loretta. He had been with the woman for three years before Leanne had sunken her claws into him. What's even worst is that when she had stolen him, Loretta was pregnant with his child.

Loretta was a cosmetologist who often did Leanne's hair at her house. They weren't necessarily friends, but they had held many conversations. Loretta didn't allow many of her customers in her house. But she trusted Leanne for some unknown reason.

She was so depressed after Levi left her. She committed suicide two months after giving birth to her son, Levi Jr., all alone in the hospital. It was one thing for Levi to leave her, but to abandon their son, too, was more than she could handle. Jamie's father had every intention of being there for Loretta during the birth of their child, but Jamie's mother didn't give him the message like she'd said she would when Loretta called to tell him that she was in labor. She lied and told him that Loretta had called her and told her that she could have the ole fool because he wasn't none of her son's father anyway.

Levi was angry with Loretta when he thought that she had betrayed him. But when he saw Levi for the first time, sitting in his grandmother's lap at Loretta's funeral, he knew that he was his son. Subsequently, he went into a deep depression himself after realizing he hadn't been there for Loretta during the birth of their son. He became an alcoholic, drinking day and night to keep himself from thinking about how he had caused a woman who had always been there for him to take her own life. Soon thereafter, he started to beat on Jamie's mother. He resented her, but couldn't really blame her because he had made the decision to sleep with her. She was hell bent on sleeping with him in Loretta's bed. He should have known that if she would do that, she would definitely lie to keep him all to herself.

Leanne finally got the strength to leave him after he'd dislocated her shoulder in a domestic dispute when Jamie was four-years-old. He then began a cycle of living off one woman after another and then another. The last woman that he had was a twenty-one-year-old girl named Analyn from Quezon City in the Philippines. She couldn't speak much English. But she was willing to cater to him until he died. He died when Jamie was seventeen-years-old from cirrhosis of the liver. He'd drank himself into an early grave. Leanne didn't bother to go to his funeral. Jamie didn't see the need to go either.

He had written her off at the precise moment that her mother written him off. But he'd come to the same school that she attended to pick up the children of the women that he was courting. When her mother called her up to tell her of his death, she responded. "Well, that's too bad. Do you think you can stop by Wal-Mart on your way home from work and get me a three-way poster board, please? I have a science project that I need to be working on."

The doorbell rang. Jamie ignored it, pouring herself a third glass of scotch. It was Vincent's day to pick Amina up from daycare and she was going to spend the night with him as well. So, she could get as tore up as she wanted to. She wasn't going to be anywhere but in her bed anyway. The doorbell rang again.

"Who is it?!" Jamie yelled as she forced herself out of bed and staggered down the stairs. She opened the door without looking through the peephole. "Aren't you supposed to be at work?" She asked Vincent when she saw him standing on her porch.

Vincent dropped his jaw, obviously shocked. He followed Jamie into the house and closed the door behind him. It was only twelve noon, and Jamie was beyond being able to function intoxicated. He walked over to her.

"Are you trying to be a naughty boy?" She asked, tussling to take off her clothes.

"Don't do that." Vincent said trying to keep Jamie from disrobing in the foyer.

"Oh, so you don't want my poo-nanny no more, huh?" She said, poking her lip out, pretending to be pouting. Vincent reached out to grab her just in time for her to fall into his arms, vomiting in his lap.

Tamyra Walker

"Did I just do that?" Jamie asked looking at Vincent with big sad eyes.

Chapter 16

It was a beautiful day to Vincent. The last thing he was going to do was to spend it being stuck inside and that included at home and at work. "Maybe I'll chill with my boys who I haven't seen in a while." He said to himself, as he popped his Tupac, 'All eyes on me' cd into his disc changer. An hour or so later, Vincent parked his Ford F-150 in Jamie's driveway and walked up to her doorway. His homies weren't available. He had nowhere else to go. So, he decided he would see what Jamie was up too. Really he didn't want to go back home. It wasn't just that it was such a beautiful day- that he didn't want to be there. Truthfully speaking, he'd just awaken from a gruesome nightmare where something really crazy was happening to him and he didn't know why. He just wanted a friendly face to look at and since he had totally ruined things with his fiancé, Alese, he thought that maybe Jamie would listen to him since they had been getting along a little over the past few weeks.

He knocked on the door. He knew that she had to be there because he had talked to her earlier when she dropped their daughter off at daycare. He agreed that he would pick Amina up and allow her to spend the night with him as well. But then his sister, Malina, called and asked if Amina could spend the night with her and her son

Carmichael, since they were in town. He didn't think Jamie would mind. But to be sure, he was going to ask her while he was at her house. If she even let him in. Their last get together hadn't gone the way he'd expected when his best friend, Marlena, showed up acting a fool.

"I was just mad, Vincent. You went through a lot with that ole hood rat. I didn't want you to be caught up in her deceitful web anymore. You deserve better than that." That was what Marlena had told him when he asked her why she acted the way that she did. But he knew it was more to it than what she said. Besides, she knew just as well as he did that he was the one who had dogged Jamie out. All Jamie had ever done was be nice to him. Marlena and Donna had upheld him in all of his wrongdoing. They were far away from being real friends, although he knew he wouldn't have listened to them if they had told him he was wrong when he was doing his dirt.

Vincent waited a few minutes and knocked on the door again. A minute or so later, Jamie opened the door and she was the last way he'd ever expected to see her- intoxicated beyond the point of being able to function. He walked towards her because he was afraid that she was going to fall on her face. He caught her just in time for her to throw up in his lap.

"Ewwwwwwww!" He grimaced, fighting the urge to vomit himself. He had never been in her new house yet. In fact, she hadn't even gotten any new living room furniture. She had given her old living room set to her sister, Janna, and was expecting Haverty's to deliver her new sectional and dining room set to her new home in a couple of days. Vincent knew that she had her bedroom set put together upstairs. He gently carried her limp body up the stairs and gathered her some clothes to put her in the shower. He could have had sex with her right then if he had wanted to. But he didn't want it from her if she wasn't aware. He wanted her to consent. He was pretty sure that she would eventually. He'd put it on her too well in the past for her to keep playing the little game she was playing. She was trying to act like she didn't want it just as badly as he did.

When he had gotten her cleaned up and in some more clothes he went downstairs and grabbed a pair of gym shorts and a t-shirt out of his truck. As he went to walk back up the driveway, a big black Hummer sped past him, almost running him over. "The fuck?!" He said as he bent down to catch his breath after having to run for his life. He didn't get a glimpse of the person in the Hummer because the windows were dark and whoever it was never stopped or even slowed down. He took a long hot shower in Jamie's downstairs bathroom and returned upstairs afterwards with some hot tea.

"How the hell did you get in my house?" Jamie asked him when she saw him walking into her bedroom.

"You let me in." He mumbled. "Here, drink this. And here is a glass of water and some extra strength Tylenol. You need to take two. I know your head ought to be killing you."

"It is." She said, grimacing from the pain.

"What the hell is going on, Jamie?" Vincent then asked her. "And, please don't tell me nothing. You never even got this drunk after we fell out with each other."

Jamie sucked her teeth.

"I don't remember us falling out with each other, Vincent. I remember your lying ass having a fiancé that I didn't know anything about. Don't try to water the shit down."

Vincent put his hand up, "Okay, so I did you wrong. Is that what you want to hear? I admit to it, I dogged you out, really good, Jamie Ferrell." He paused to see what her reaction would be. When she didn't respond he continued.

"But, even after I dogged you out, you didn't go getting sloppy drunk like this."

"Well, I couldn't." Jamie yelled. "I was pregnant with your child, idiot."

"Even if you weren't pregnant, Jamie, you wouldn't have gotten yourself intoxicated like this. So, will you please cut the bullshit and tell me what the hell is going on?"

Jamie took a deep breath, and placed both of her hands over her face.

"I don't want to talk about it, Vincent."

"Why not?" He asked, pushing the issue.

"Because it's none of your damn business, that's why." She yelled to the top of her lungs. "Why don't you tell me what you are here for, huh?"

Vincent felt himself getting angry. He stood and walked over to the window to look out and to calm himself down. He saw that same black hummer, through the shrubbery in Jamie's front yard passing by her house, but this time at a normal pace.

"Aye." He said, as he turned to look back at Jamie. "You might want to be careful when you are going to your car. Apparently there are some non-driving motherfucker's living in this neighborhood."

Jamie rolled her eyes.

"Whatever Vincent."

"I'm serious." He said. "Some dude in a black hummer almost ran me over when I went out to my truck to get some clean clothes.

Tamyra Walker

"A black hummer?!" Jamie gasped with her eyes wide, as she dropped the mug that she had been nursing on the floor. Hot tea splashed on both of her bare feet and she yelled out in pain."

"Are you, okay?" Vincent ran over to make sure she hadn't cut herself. She was sitting on the floor crying, and trembling uncontrollably.

"He's never going to leave me alone." She said almost inaudibly. "I moved out of the apartment and into my own house, and he still found me. He's never going to leave me alone. I just want him to leave me alone."

"Who found you, Jamie? Who won't leave you alone? Don't do that, now. Come on, you got to tell me. I cannot help you if you won't tell me. Who the fuck won't leave you alone, Jamie? Vincent shook Jamie repeatedly, trying to get her to talk to him. But to no avail. She continued crying hysterically. Eventually he gave up. He stood, grabbed his gym bag off the bed and darted down the stairs in a flash. He slammed the door as he left out of the house and sped off up the street like a mad man.

Several hours later, Vincent stormed into his condo. He had been sitting out in the hot sun for a couple of hours after he left Jamie's house trying to get a tail on this guy who wouldn't leave her alone. He knew she was an emotional person. But he didn't think that she was as emotional as she let on earlier. He really believed that she was partially putting on to avoid telling him who the hell the guy was in the Hummer. But he was going to find out. And when he found out, he was going to kill the guy if it came to it. He hadn't done right by Jamie. He knew that she wasn't his woman. But she did have his child. If he had to die in the process, he was going to make sure his daughter, Amina, was taken care of and that she wasn't in any danger.

Vincent went to sleep a couple hours later, watching his favorite television show, *Breaking bad*. He fell into a deep slumber and immediately started having the nightmare that had been haunting him for quite a while. He remembered someone putting something in his drink that had him knocked out cold. An hour or so later, he was lying naked on a bed in a hotel. A few minutes later he'd felt a woman riding him. She jumped up and down on his manhood like her life depended on it. He enjoyed how she gyrated her hips in a circular motion. One thing that he could say was that she wasn't like anyone else he had ever been with before. He couldn't see her face, even after trying. But he could hear her moaning in his ear, telling him that soon enough she would be his woman.

Her voice sounded very familiar. But he was so blown by the great sex that he wasn't trying to figure out who she was. He tried to push her off him when he felt himself about to ejaculate, but she'd said, "No, squirt in me, baby. Give me all of your love." He tried to control himself but a couple minutes later he exploded inside of her. She laid her head over on his chest and whispered, "That's it, baby. You fucked me just right, daddy." Then suddenly she started to bleed, heavily. She panicked and said. "I'm losing the baby. I'm miscarrying our baby." Blood was pouring out of her vagina faster than water on the highest level out of a spigot. "I'm losing the baby, Vincent." She kept saying over and over again…"

Vincent sat up in the middle of his bed, breathing heavily. "Why do I keep having this dream?" He said. He turned to take a sip of the stale water that was sitting on his night table. He couldn't understand why he was so young in the dream. He couldn't have been no more than eighteen or nineteen-years-old. He slapped his hand against his forehead, trying hard to piece things together. He was almost certain that the dream was something that had actually happened in real life. *But that can't be the case, though. I'm not stupid. Hell, I would've known if I had gotten someone pregnant or not.* He racked his brain trying to remember who was even pregnant when he was that age. He was about to lay back down after being unsuccessful and then Donna's face flashed right before his eyes.

Chapter 17

'It's not easy being me out in this messed up world. I've been through a lot. But all would be well if I didn't have to deal with that no good man laid up at my house right now. I need my love, Vincent. I've been sweet on him seems like forever and the feeling just won't go away. This friend crap is getting hard. I want my man… and if I cannot have him, that ole bitch, Jamie, won't have him either'

~ Donna Kilpatrick ~

~*~

Donna and Marlena were together at the Rendezvous night club, drinking heavily, still up to their usual same ole same ole. It was two am. They decided to end the night with breakfast at the Waffle House.

"Let me check in with Marcus." Donna said to Marlena. She whipped out her cellular phone, noticing that she had a text message from someone. *Oh, his annoying behind already checking up with me.* She thought as she opened the text and saw Vincent's name as the sender. Immediately, she felt her pulse increase. She was excited, deciding she should go outside to read the text message.

"I'll be back." She said to Marlena, hurriedly walking out the door before she had time to ask her any questions.

173

Tamyra Walker

She stood by her Kia Sorento and opened the text message and read it aloud. "I need to talk to you." Closing the text, she decided that she would call him to see what was up. Before she had time to dial his number, Marcus beeped in.

"Hey, bae." She answered, excited because Vincent had sent her a text message, not because Marcus was on the phone.

"Where the hell your ass at?" He asked, puffing on a cigarette.

Donna immediately became annoyed.

"Didn't I tell your ass that I was going to the club, with Marlena?"

"You ain't at no club, bitch." He said, taking another pull off the cigarette. "Now I'm going to ask you one more time and one more time, only- WHERE THE HELL ARE YOU?" His voice was loud enough to raise the roof on the building.

"You are really starting to get on my nerves, Marcus." Donna yelled. "We just left the damn club. We are at the Waffle House now. I'm hungry, okay? Is that a problem with you? Can a bitch eat, please?"

"Don't get smart with me."

"Man, ain't nobody getting smart with you. I wasn't even thinking about you, if you want me to be honest."

"Keep talking, and I'm going to stick my foot up your behind. You need to have your ass back at this house in the next hour."

Donna sucked her teeth. The signal was lost for a few seconds. She tried to call Marcus back. But before she could, the phone rang in her hand.

"Did you hang up in my face?" Marcus asked with his voice elevated. He had told Donna about hanging the phone up in his face.

"I did not hang up on you. This raggedy ass Alcatel phone you bought from Metro PC doesn't keep a signal and you know that. If your cheap ass had gotten me that iPhone that I asked for, you wouldn't have to worry about this. So be mad at yourself, ole penny pinching ass, nigga."

"Whatever." He said, coughing from the cigarette smoke. "Bring me a patty melt combo. And, stop and get a box of magnums. I want some tonight."

"Yeah, okay." Donna said, trying hard to get him off the phone.

"And a sack from my boy Raymond on Harrison Street."

"Okay." Donna repeated herself. Marcus hung up without saying anything else.

"Damn, scrub." Donna mumbled as she dialed Vincent's number.

"Where are you?" He asked, answering the phone.

"I'm at the Waffle House, over by the club. Come chill with your girl."

"Yeah, okay." He said. "I'll be there in ten minutes. I got something to talk to you about."

****

Jamie walked downstairs dressed in a pair of tight fitting jeans and a spaghetti strapped t-shirt. She stepped into her flip-flops sitting by her front door. She walked to the back door, set the alarm, and disappeared into the garage. As she backed her Infiniti out of the driveway, she stopped at the mailbox to retrieve her mail. She put the SUV in park while briefly sorting through the mail. A big smile emerged across her face when she saw the graduation invitation from her friend, Teresa. They hadn't been hanging out or talking to each other much since before Amina was born. Now she knew why. Teresa had finally decided to finish those last couple of semesters of college she had been dragging her feet on and would be graduating in August with a Bachelor's degree in Social Work.

"I'm so proud of you, boo." Jamie said out loud, as if Teresa was in the truck with her and could hear what she was saying. She put the invitation in her glove compartment and took off down the street. She hadn't had a chance to really go grocery shopping yet since moving into her new home. Since Amina was spending the night with her aunt,

Malina, she decided to ride through the city a little bit to clear her mind.

An hour later when she was preparing to come back home, she stopped by the Waffle House next to the Rendezvous club, the club that she used to frequent with Teresa and Elaine, back in the day when they were fresh out of high school and all cool with each other. She hadn't had a double order of hash browns scattered, smothered, covered, and chunked, in several months and was craving for them the way she did when she was in her first trimester of pregnancy with Amina. She walked into the Waffle House, immediately hearing arguing going on at the other end of the little diner.

"So, you just decided to put something in my drink, bitch? Fuck me, get yourself pregnant, miscarry the baby, and you didn't think that I had a right to know about *any* of it?!" Everybody in the diner was tuned into the conversation, including the cook and the servers.

"That sounds like Vincent." Jamie said as she turned to look in the direction of the arguing.

Her mouth dropped wide open when she saw him with his finger pointed in Donna's face, yelling at her. She looked like she could have hidden herself under anything that would have safeguarded her from the embarrassment she obviously felt knowing that a secret that she tried to keep under wraps for so long was finally exposed.

177

"I'm sorry, Vincent!" Donna yelled back. "You were paying all these other bitches attention. You acted like you didn't notice me. I been down with you since day one and you never thought to notice that maybe you should have given us a chance to be in love." She was sobbing uncontrollably.

Vincent wasn't thinking clearly. He was so angry. He drew back his hand.

"Don't you dare hit her, Vincent. Otherwise, your ass is going to jail." Jamie said as she rushed over to him. She stood in between him and Donna to keep him from getting himself in trouble. "Think about Amina... take a deep breath."

He turned to look at Jamie. He took her advice, smiling just a little as he thought about his daughter. He loved her and couldn't imagine himself sitting behind bars. That would cause him to miss out on valuable time with her.

"What are you doing here this time of the morning, Jamie?"

"Well, if it ain't super save a whore." Marlena sneered. She glared at Jamie like she was waiting for the right moment to attack her.

"Excuse me?" Donna yelled. "Fuck why she is here! We were talking about our baby that we lost." Donna glared at Jamie and rolled her eyes. "She need to take her little high and mighty, prissy behind on back to whatever rock she crawled from under."

Jamie took a couple of steps back and put both of her hands up. She took a couple of deep breaths, deciding not to say to Donna what she really wanted to say.

"A baby that I didn't know about... a baby that you drugged me to get. What kind of desperate ass bitch does some foul mess like that? But I guess that's what I get. I mean, I knew you two were grimy. I just didn't think that applied when it came to me... you're supposed to be boy."

Donna rolled her eyes.

"You ain't got to be telling that ole stinky bitch all of our business, Vincent. This is between me and you." Marlena was speechless. But she was going to have a few choice words with Donna when she pulled herself together. How could she claim to be her best friend and had kept all of this information from her. And how could she violate the code. They both had agreed that Vincent was off limits to either one of them, even though she'd been planning how to get him for herself the past few weeks. She was both surprised, and hurt that Donna had already had him.

Tamyra Walker

Jamie turned to walk away. But turned back around to face Vincent when she heard him defending her to his friends for the first time since she had met him.

"Don't call the mother of my child, a bitch. She has never done anything to you. And I don't plan to ever tell your scandalous ass that again." Vincent was in her face again. But he didn't raise his hand to hit her. He wasn't going to stoop that low, although he wanted to slap her so hard and watch her whole face rotate.

Donna sucked her teeth and waved her hand.

"Nigga, you just want some pussy! You ain't slick." She looked at Jamie and rolled her eyes again. "Alese left your ass. So, now you want to play lovey dovey with the hoe you laughed at and talked about to me and Marlena." She looked at Jamie and spat, "Hell yeah he talked about you, bitch. He never wanted you from the get go. He was just using your ass."

Vincent clapped his hands.

"Your dry snitch game is on point, boo. I'll give you that. But one thing is for sure- I don't have to drug anybody to get sex. You must know yourself that shit you got between your legs that you throw at any nigga that's willing to give your thirsty behind a dollar, ain't worth the fuck." He backed away from her slowly before saying, "I'm done with both of you. Do not call me again. Ever. Either one of you." He grabbed Jamie by the hand and tore out of the tiny diner.

Jamie opened her mouth to speak.

"Please, don't ask me any questions," Vincent said. "Get your butt in the truck and go home. I'll be right behind you."

Tamyra Walker

Chapter 18

'God has been good to me. He has blessed me to have the finer things in life. I have a wonderful husband, a thriving catering business, and the best daughter any mother could ask for. My sweet, darling, Janna, gives me life. She is everything I could have asked for and more. Jamie will never be her. She is one mistake that I wish I hadn't made'

~ Leanne Marshall ~

~*~

"Leanne, we are going to be late if you don't come down those stairs, right now." Bill, Janna's father, and Jamie's stepfather paced the hardwood living room floor impatiently for a couple of minutes before walking out of the four bedroom, ranch-style house.

The white house, adorned with black shingles, with the small cottage in the back yard that they had rented out to a young couple was nestled on two acres of land. It was amidst a myriad of trees, flower gardens, two ponds, and a gazebo. Bill walked down the sidewalk to start the engine to their brand new, straight off the car lot, Cadillac Deville. It purred to life. He sat still, in his navy slacks and navy and white collar shirt. Sweat trickled down his forehead as he turned the

AC on in the car. He pulled his Cuban cigar out of his pocket and lit it. He inhaled deeply, determined to rid himself of the ill thoughts that he was having towards his wife… who he'd once adored, but nowadays he sometimes couldn't stand the sight of her. The very thing he loved about her was now what he was starting to not love about her. Her captivating beauty had stunned him. He knew that he had to have her when he first laid eyes on her. He couldn't believe that she'd said 'yes' when he had finally gotten the nerve to ask her out. Soon thereafter, they were an item, and he always had her on his arm. He was happy to show her off to his friends… but he regarded her as more than just a beautiful trophy. He genuinely loved her and wanted nothing more than to spend the rest of his life catering to her.

"A woman that beautiful deserves to be catered to." He often said about her. His first marriage had failed only after three-and-a-half-years. And, after a two-year hiatus from doing what he once called, "the relationship thing," he'd decided to give love another shot.

As Bill sat there, his mind going haywire, he took a couple more pulls off his cigar. He retrieved his personalized stainless steel flask from his glove compartment, taking a swig of the Seagram's extra dry Gin.

His mind reflected back to the day when he first met Leanne. It was a summer's night in the middle of July, 1985. He'd done his last bid in the Army and decided not to reenlist. He sat in Winston's Bar on the West side of town, having himself a shot of whiskey. He had his back turned to the door but he could see Leanne when she waltzed into the bar, through the mirror on the wall. He stopped talking mid-sentence as she sashayed over to a table in the back of the bar and sat down. She was 5 feet, 7 inches tall, thick in the legs and thighs and had a butt that stood firmly like it was saluting his Lieutenant. She wore a sleeveless peach dress that came a couple inches above her knees. Her hair was long and silky. It flowed down her back. The soft curls that she wore were flipped at the ends. She was gorgeous. There was no other word to describe her. He wished he could freeze that moment in time. Little did he know, she'd set the whole shenanigan up for him to meet her. A friend of hers had told her that he had a few coins in the bank, and she jumped all over the notion of having him for herself, like a bitch in heat.

"Oh, I see you got your eyes on a little hottie." Bill's friend, JC, whispered just low enough for him to hear. Bill didn't respond. He continued watching Leanne until she looked up and started to watch him as well.

Daaaaaaaaamn. Was his only thought. He turned around on his barstool and stared at her even harder. She smiled and waved at him. He was too stunned to do anything but continue to stare at her.

184

"Those were the good ole days." Bill said as he took one last swig of the Gin before closing the top on the flask and placing it back into his glove compartment. They were supposed to be meeting Janna at her apartment so that they could start planning her and Pernell's wedding. It would also be the first time that either one of them met Pernell's family. Leanne wanted to make a good impression, as always. She heard that Pernell's mother was bringing her so-called famous peach cobbler. She didn't want to be outdone. So she made a batch of red velvet petit fours, placing them underneath the finest crystal cake pan that she had in her cabinet.

Leanne had always won first place in their church's annual baking contest with her petit fours. As well, Janna constantly bragged to her friends about how good they were. So, she knew that they would be a hit, the perfect strategy to woo herself into the hearts of Pernell's family. As much as she didn't accept her own daughter, Jamie, it was important to her to be accepted by any and every one that she came in contact with. That was especially the case with the in-laws of the daughter she'd invested so much time into pruning to be her trophy child.

"I'm coming!" She yelled in her unusually cheery but condescending voice. She sprayed a little more of her Gucci Bamboo perfume around her neck and looked her face over one last time to make sure her make-up was the way it should be. She had made a point a long time ago to never leave the house without her face looking its very best. And thanks to plastic surgery, she didn't have any crow's feet around her eyes like a couple of her acquaintances did. She tried hard not to judge them, though. She knew that everyone wasn't blessed to live high on the hog the way that she did.

Leanne smiled at her face. She knew that Bill was a little impatient. "He'll just have to wait." She smirked as she sashayed down the stairs, put the alarm on and joined her husband at last in the car.

"It took you long enough." He said, putting the car in drive. "You must've had to make the make-up, honey?"

"Whatever, Bill." Leanne replied. "Not all of us have the luxury of shaving a few hairs off of our face and looking totally fabulous."

Bill shook his head at his wife. He had no idea that she would be so vain at almost fifty-three years of age.

"Sooooo." She said, trying hard to strike up a conversation with her husband, but he wasn't really in the mood for friendly conversation.

She pursed her lips, glaring at him for a couple of minutes.

"Are you going to sit here like a big moose and pout, or are you going to tell me what is wrong with you?" She finally asked, pulling the sun visor down to keep the sun from getting in her eyes. She had forgotten her Ray Ban sunglasses and didn't feel like asking Bill to turn around to go back and get them. She had already had enough of his attitude over the past week to last a lifetime. She didn't know how much more she could take.

"Grown ass man, acting like a big baby." she mumbled under her breath.

"Tell me something, Leanne." Bill said. He turned to look at her when they were sitting still at a red light.

She took a deep breath.

"What is it, Bill?"

"Why do you treat Jamie the way you do?"

Her eyes began to twitch the way they did when she was angry.

"And, how do I treat her, dear?" She asked, pretending to be clueless. "Care to enlighten me?"

"Don't run that game on me, Leanne. You know damn well what I am talking about."

"I'll tell you what I do know, honey." Leanne said sarcastically, looking straight ahead. "The light is green and you need to drive."

He took his foot off the brake and sped up the road.

"Jamie is your child, your own flesh and blood. Hell, I treat her better than you do. I don't understand, Leanne. You don't treat Janna that way."

"It's not for you to understand, Bill." She said, struggling even harder to disguise her anger. "The last time I checked, Jamie's birth certificate said that I was her mother, and that Levi Clinton Ferrell was her father." She paused to note Bill's reaction. He was chewing the inside of his jaw to keep from going off on Leanne the way he wanted too.

"So, what *that* means is that you don't have anything to do with how I treat *my* daughter, sweetheart." She paused again, feeling like those words that she'd already spoken needed to marinate in his brain before she continued.

He looked at her with fire in his eyes. She ignored him and spoke again.

"So, unless you want to find yourself on the couch tonight, sir... I think you'd better pull your nose out of my business."

Bill slammed on brakes, as the next light turned yellow... and then red. Leanne huffed, "You can barely drive right these days, but you want to worry about my daughter. I gave birth to her, not you. And, I didn't say anything to her little sensitive behind that she didn't need to hear. But, oh no. You want to treat her like a spoiled little brat." Leanne threw her hands while speaking. Her behavior mimicked that of a teenager. "Humph, I bet she don't even know who the father is to that poor child that she went and had out of wedlock."

"Well, I guess she was just following in her mother's footsteps." Bill yelled over her. "You weren't married when you gave birth to her. And, we weren't married when Janna was born, although I asked your stubborn behind to marry me before you even got pregnant. If my memory serves me right, we didn't say, 'I do' until Janna was almost three-years-old."

"And! What's your point?" Leanne asked, tapping her foot, and filing her fingernails. She was really starting to lose her patience with him. *He has a lot of nerve to question me about anything. Jamie is my daughter. That means I can say what I damn well please to her.* She thought.

"So, that means you had *two* babies out of wedlock. Now, what makes you think you can judge Jamie for doing the same thing that you did? Don't you think that's kind of hypocritical, love? Do you even know what hypocritical means? What kind of example did you set for her, honey?"

Leanne pulled her ear buds out of her Coach bag and put them in her ears. She refused to say anything else to Bill. She was going to listen to Chaka Khan's greatest hits and tune his interfering behind out.

Tamyra Walker

She had never stooped so low as to explain herself to him in the twenty years that they had been married. She wasn't about to start now. "He can just get out of his feelings and shut his fat trap… especially if he expects me to cook his ungrateful behind any dinner tonight." She snorted under her breath.

Chapter 19

Janna ran through her apartment like a mad woman, making sure everything was in order for her parents and her fiancé's parents who would all be arriving momentarily. She still only worked part time as a cashier at Publix's. She sold Mary Kay make-up when she had time and had been helping Mr. Ogletree, a Deacon at her church, and a prominent divorce attorney with some typing that he paid her to do. It's not like she had a lot of money floating around. But she was going to show her guests what hospitality was all about. She had a little nest egg stashed aside that she dibbed in for this occasion. Pernell had given her half of the money she would need to make sure everything was the way it should be.

Janna walked over to her counter in the kitchen and pressed play on her IPOD. She sang along with Anita Baker. "Ain't no need in worrying what the night is going to bring. It'll be all over in the morning."

While Anita's sultry voice filled the air, she removed the chocolate chip cookies from the grocery bag, rearranging them on a crystal cookie platter that Jamie bought for her when they were out shopping one Saturday afternoon. Jamie had always taken good care of her. Her parents paid half of her rent. They had no idea that Jamie was paying the other half. She didn't want her to have a thing to stress about. She just wanted her to do as well as she possibly could in school so that she could have a career, never having to live paycheck to paycheck the way she witnessed so many other people who had to settle for the low paying jobs because they hadn't chased higher education.

A loud knock on the door startled Janna. She washed her hands, hurriedly walking to the door. A big broad smile covered her lips when she peeped through the peep hole and saw her parents standing there, and not empty handed. They came bearing gifts.

"Mom, you didn't have to do this." Janna said to her mother, reaching out to take the cake pan she had in her hand. "Pernell's parents are going to love these!"

"I'm sure they will." Leanne beamed, batting her eyes and walking into the apartment.

"Hey, daddy." Janna said to her father. She ran into his arms, squeezing him with all of her might. He leaned over and kissed her on the cheek.

"How is my baby girl doing," he asked.

Leanne rolled her eyes in exasperation.

"I'm doing great dad. I'm so glad you and mom are here."

"We are glad to be here, too, baby." Leanne interrupted. "Oh, honey! You have it looking so nice in here. You have great taste, hun." She looked around the twelve hundred square foot apartment, adoring the abstract art on the wall. Her stiletto's played a tune of excitement against the tiled floor as she walked from the foyer to the living room. She gasped. "Where did you get this nice living room set? Sheesh, I don't even have a set this nice in my house."

Janna smiled weakly. Although she was more than pleased to see her parents, she was upset because she hadn't been able to get in contact with Jamie. She'd left her a message letting her know about the meeting that she was holding to start planning the wedding. But Jamie didn't bother to respond. She knew that her sudden disappearance had everything to do with their mother. It was hard for Janna to pretend like everything was okay when she was certain her mother had to know that she had been very offensive to Jamie.

"Thanks, mom. I got this living room set from Jamie." She plopped down on the barely used couch while her mother continued roaming her apartment.

"Oh, I see." Leanne said, suddenly turning her nose up and opting to sit at the dining room table. She took off her heels and expelled a deep breath.

Tamyra Walker

"Mom, I got the dining room table from Jamie, too. So, if you think the living room set is disgusting because it came from my sister-your daughter... then the dining room set is just as filthy. Wouldn't you think?"

Bill cracked a smile at his daughter from the barstool he sat on at the counter. He was proud of her for putting her mother in her place. He nodded his head at her when she glanced over at him.

But Leanne wasn't too thrilled. She rose to her feet and lunged at Janna. She grabbed her by her chin and forced her to look at her. Bill stood too.

"You better not hit her, Leanne." He said with authority in his voice. "She didn't say anything to you that your sensitive behind didn't need to hear." He said, mocking what she had said to him a little while ago in the car.

Leanne ignored him. "Don't you ever speak to me like that. Do you hear me? What exactly are you insinuating?"

Tears rolled down Janna's cheeks.

"Mom, I am not insinuating anything. Everybody noticed what a bih.. I mean how you treated Jamie last Saturday."

Leanne's mouth dropped open at the fact that her youngest daughter, the daughter that she had always revered and loved with all of her heart was about to call her a bitch. Her eyes welled up with tears. But for once, Janna wasn't moved by her tears. She didn't care how she felt. It was hard for her to believe that she had any feelings at all if she could be so mean to her own child for no reason.

"I don't like the way you treat Jamie, mom. I don't understand..."

"This is not the time for us to be discussing this nonsense, Janna." Leanne pulled a Kleenex from her purse and dabbed at her eyes.

"Now, I stopped at Williamson Bridal a few days ago and picked up a few booklets." She looked up to notice that Janna had a disgusted expression on her face. "I, ugh, marked a few wedding gowns that I thought would look good on you. But, of course you have the last say so, sweetie."

Leanne peered again at her youngest daughter, saddened that she had put her hands on her violently. She assumed that Jamie had to be filling her head up with lies because she had never talked to her like that before. She had always been respectful. That's why Leanne loved her so much. She was perfect. Her father was perfect. Well, he had been until recently when he decided to question her about everything. She couldn't understand what his problem was. He should've just appreciated having a wife who cared enough to always look her very best on his arm. She could still handle her business in the bedroom and as far as she knew, all of his needs were satisfied. There was no need for him to go stirring the pot worrying about something that was frankly none of his business.

Janna turned away from her mother, sadly walking to the back of her apartment. She was glad that Pernell and his parents hadn't arrived yet. She would be so embarrassed for them to know that her mother could be downright hateful for no reason. Of course, she had always tried to portray herself as sweet as pie, but her venom had become more widespread and lethal in the past month or so. Janna honestly didn't know how much more she could take.

As she picked up her cellular phone off her night table, she wondered had she really been that naïve or was it that she didn't want to see the truth written in bold letters before her eyes. Her mother had never mistreated her. She wondered if she unconsciously failed to care before that Jamie was being mistreated, because it wasn't her.

Taking a deep breath, Janna dialed Jamie's number. The voice mail immediately came on.

"Look, Jamie." Janna solemnly spoke to her sister's voicemail. "Please call me."

Chapter 20

"I don't know what else to say to you. I...I... honestly don't even know if you are okay or not." Janna's frustrated voice rang through Jamie's voicemail. "I have been trying to keep a level head here, but, ugh- it's kind of hard for me not to think that you are angry with me because of what mom said."

Jamie rolled her eyes at that comment, as she lay in bed on top of her Duvet cover listening to Janna pour her heart out.

"Look, Jamie. We need to talk." She paused for a second. "If you are there Jamie, please pick up." Another brief pause filled the air. Janna sighed heavily. "Fine, Jamie. When you get this message, please call me." She disconnected the call without saying anything else.

Jamie picked up the remote lying next to her on the king-sized bed and turned the television off. She knew that she was being a tad bit selfish. But even so, she didn't want to think about it at that moment. She honestly felt that since she would never be her mother's golden child, she had earned her right to at least be selfish. *Janna can never do anything wrong... and I can never do anything right. Go figure.* Jamie's thoughts were on duty, speaking to her mind.

Tamyra Walker

"I'll call her later…" She said in reference to her sister's phone call. She turned over in bed, folded one of her pillows in half on top of another and instantly fell asleep. She was sleeping soundly until Vincent woke her up, crawling his rock hard body into bed next to her. That man was like a sculpture… one that Jamie never got tired of admiring.

"Where have you been? With some other woman, I bet." Jamie's voice was heavy with sleep as she found the strength to turn and look him in the face.

"Go back to sleep, Jamie." He said as she settled her soft body into his arms.

"I don't want no shit out of you, Vincent." She closed her eyes and attempted to drift back off to sleep. She and Vincent had been sneaking around, having sex with each other for nearly two weeks now. It started the morning she walked into the Waffle House only to find him battling it out with his two best friends, Donna and Marlena.

Jamie couldn't believe what her ears were hearing. She caught up to him just in time to tell him, "Vincent if you hit her, you are going your ass to jail." He had his hand drawn back as if he was thinking about punching Donna right in the center of her nose. *I'd pay big bucks to see that.* Her thoughts weren't as kind as the words she actually spoke to Vincent.

Slowly Vincent lowered his hand, rethinking the whole situation. He backed away but not before saying, "I'm done with both of you. Do not call me again. Ever. Either one of you."

Both Marlena and Donna's mouth flew open in disbelief as he said those words to them. Marlena looked like she would break down and cry, while Donna tried to intimidate Jamie by shooting her eye daggers.

When he stormed out of the diner, Vincent grabbed her by the hand, ordering her to get in her truck and go home. He assured her that he would be right behind her. Jamie nodded her head, meticulously walking to her truck with all kinds of thoughts running through her mind. A few miles away from her home, she glanced in her rearview mirror. Sure enough, Vincent was right behind her just as he said he would be.

She turned right onto Joyce circle, pulling into the third driveway on the left. Reaching upward, she pressed the button clipped on her sun visor. The garage promptly opened. She pressed down on the gas just slightly pulling her truck in. She pushed the button again, opening the other side of her garage. Vincent followed suit, pulling his truck into her garage. They sat, parked next to each other for a couple of minutes, twilling their thumbs, sneaking glances whenever they thought the other wasn't watching.

Tamyra Walker

Finally, Jamie opened the door to her truck and got out. She walked slowly intentionally to her back door, trying hard to control the thoughts that were horse playing with her emotions. *It's nearly three in the morning. Amina is with his sister. What could we possibly have to talk about?*

As she put her hand on the doorknob, she felt Vincent standing closely behind her. She inhaled and exhaled slowly when he touched the small of her back, gently pushing her forward into the house.

Jamie flipped on the lights in the kitchen and placed her purse on the counter. "So, what's up, Vincent?" She asked after she poured herself a glass of wine. She turned it up immediately, drinking every drop, before pouring herself a second glass. She needed to calm down and wine tended to do that for her. She grabbed the remote to her Bose wave stereo system and allowed Sade's voice to melt all of her tension's away. The lyrics to *This is No Ordinary Love* soothed her and at the same time made her feel a little uncomfortable.

Vincent smiled, knowing what she was thinking. He leaned over on the counter, staring at her as if he'd never had a good look at her before. She sat Indian-styled on the sofa, too afraid to look him in his eyes. She was beautiful, even dressed down with no makeup on. *Maybe if she had come my way in another lifetime, I wouldn't have had to break her heart.* He thought, Erykah Badu's song running rampant through his mind. He had never intended to hurt her. But what she wanted wasn't what he had wanted. He knew that he had been selfish. But she was looking finger licking good to him on the subway that day, crying her eyes out over another dude who'd done her wrong. He had to step to her. He wouldn't have been a man if he hadn't. He had to write his name on her walls. He was sure it would be one that she would never forget. He had to have a piece of her pie and he would never lie to anyone and say that it wasn't appetizing in exactly the way that he had expected it to be.

"There's beer in the fridge." Jamie spoke, pretending not to notice how he was looking at her. She could feel the side of her face burning. She knew that it was because Vincent was watching her every move.

He walked over to the refrigerator and grabbed a Budweiser. "Thanks." He said.

Jamie simply nodded her head.

"When did you start drinking Budweiser?" He asked, knowing that she didn't drink it. He was being nosy and wanted to know if she would slip and tell him that she'd had a man over. He tried to play it off as marking his territory. But truthfully speaking, he did have feelings for her, even though it was never his intentions to act on them. He was like the typical man. He didn't want to give her his heart because that would mean he would no longer get the attention from all

201

the other women that he didn't want to leave alone. At the same time, he didn't want her to give her heart to anyone else. He wanted it to be available whenever he had a taste for her. He wanted Alese, his ex-fiancé to be his main course, saving Jamie to be his dessert whenever he had a sweet tooth. Or when his main course wasn't curbing his appetite.

"You know I don't drink beer, boy." She sneered at his candor. "That's strictly for guests."

"Guests, huh?" Vincent said. "So, you were specifically thinking about me when you got this huh? Since you are well aware that I DO drink Budweiser's."

"Man, whatever." She waved her hand at him, embarrassed because she was busted.

"Humph." He said, taking a long swig from his beer. He sat the bottle on the counter before walking into the living room. "It's okay if you be thinking about me. I won't tell anybody if you don't want me to."

Jamie ignored him. *Cocky ass.* She thought to herself.

"You mind if I sit on the couch next to you?"

She nodded at the spot next to her, giving him permission to sit down. *He's trying to feel me out.* She thought, stifling a childish giggle that wanted to escape.

"Soooo, do you want to talk about what happened, a little while ago?" Jamie asked, filling the awkward silence that sung a melody to both of them.

"Nah, I don't feel like talking. I'd much rather you come on over here and lay your head on my lap."

Jamie looked at him. She opened her mouth and closed it a couple of times. But no words would come.

Vincent extended his hand to her.

"Stop acting like you don't want me, girl. I'm not going to hurt you. Your ass is tense as hell. Come on over here and let me massage you."

"Massage me?" Jamie repeated, her eyes widened.

"Your shoulders, Jamie. Let me massage your shoulders."

Jamie shook her head despondently, afraid of what she was getting herself into. Still she found herself scooting over on the couch until she could feel Vincent's flesh sending electrical currents through her body. She looked at him with innocent eyes. Vincent patted his lap. Without another thought, Jamie eased her head down in his lap and placed both of her feet up on the couch.

"Yeah, that's it." Vincent said as he leaned forward and covered Jamie's lips with his. Her lips instantly parted. He wasted no time slipping his tongue inside of her mouth. Jamie looked up to meet Vincent's eyes as a small moan escaped from a place in her heart that hadn't been touched since the last time that they had kissed. The feeling was mutual for him. He hungrily devoured her lips, gently massaged her tongue with his while twirling his fingers through her natural curls. Closing her eyes, she allowed herself to give into the feeling that was setting ablaze a fire that no one would be able to contain. She moaned again, a little louder when she felt herself getting moist. Instinctively, her legs fell apart, as if Vincent had already mounted his strong body atop hers and was about to enter her snug little sanctuary at that very moment. Almost coming on herself, she abruptly broke the kiss when she felt Vincent's hand grazing the inside of her thigh.

"We can't do this." She said, as she sat up. She stood, walking away a couple of feet and turned around to glare at him. Vincent looked at her with desire distorting his vision like cataracts. He stood also. He walked over to her slowly. She backed back a couple of steps until her back was against the wall.

"I'm serious, Vincent. I. Am. Not. Going. There. With. You."

"I missed you so much." Vincent whispered in Jamie's ear. He rubbed her back as she laid her head against his strong chest. "Did you miss me?" He asked, breaking their embrace to look at her face. That was when he saw the tears flowing freely.

"Why are you crying?" He asked, taking his hand and wiping the tears from her eyes.

"Vincent, I know you are running game on me. I can't let you hurt me again. I…I… just can't." She turned her back to him and sobbed silently. "I think you should leave." her voice choked with more tears.

Vincent walked up behind her. He gently turned her around to face him.

"I will leave Jamie. But not until I make love to you… not until I put out that fire blazing inside of you. You want me just as badly as I want you. I'm here baby…" He stepped back and pulled his polo shirt over his head. His chest was ripe with muscles. He was one who took pride in his body. And at that moment that fine body of his was making Jamie dizzy.

Vincent never took his eyes off Jamie's eyes as he reached for his belt buckle and unbuckled it. He undid his pants and gently pulled them down. Her eyes widened at the sight of his manhood. It laid, rock hard, in his black Calvin Klein boxers, waiting to be caressed or maybe even kissed.

"You see that?" He asked, taking her hands and placing them on himself. He pulled her close to him. "You did that to me, Jamie Ferrell." He whispered in her ear. "Don't leave him hanging!" He reached up, cupping her face. She intertwined her fingers between his. They stared at each a few long seconds before he tilted his head, going for her soft lips again. Jamie stood on her toes and wrapped both of her arms around his neck. They kissed passionately and didn't come up for air for five minutes or so.

"You still want me to stop?" Vincent asked, charismatically. He placed his hands under Jamie's buttocks and in one big swoop she was up in his arms. She wrapped her legs around him tightly like a child who didn't want to be put down.

"I guess that means no." Vincent groaned as he carried her back over to the couch. He yanked her leggings off and dove straight between her legs.

"Ohhhhhhhh, baby!" She said as she arched her back and raised her body up off the couch like she was in the middle of a yoga session. Her feet stayed in place like a cat who had sunken her paws into her prey.

"Oh, my, Godddddddddd!" She yelled out as he slurped on her like she was a popsicle. She took the palm of her hand and began slapping it against the couch the way a wrestler would hit the bottom of the wrestling ring when he was tapping out. He looked up at her with a stern expression on his face.

"Stop all that damn squirming, Jamie, and take it." Without another word or another second wasted, he dove, face first back into her.

"Ummmmm." She said, nodding her head but made an effort to cease the squirming. When she climaxed, he stood, stripped his boxers off, and held her legs apart while he slid as far into her as he could. He felt as if he had touched the equator of her soul as the walls of her love closed around him as if they had missed him and was showing him with a tight hug.

"Aaaaaaaaaaargh!" He yelled. "I fucking love this pussy. This shit is top shelf, baby. You got that supreme loving, baby." He held her legs further apart, stroking her slowly. He slipped out a couple of times. But Jamie quickly grabbed him and guided him back into her den of love. She buried her head in his chest and took the pounding she'd been missing. No one had been able to make her come so hard from penetration alone. But she welcomed each and every thrust, throwing it back on him at the same pace that he was giving it. When they were done, they laid on the couch, their legs intertwined. No words were said as Jamie gained composure of her breathing and fell asleep in Vincent's arms.

He really blew her mind when he took her in the shower the next day. Jamie was feeling slightly confused, not knowing what to think about their night of passion. She filled her loofah with some of the cherry scented body wash that was sitting in her shower as the thoughts flooded her mind. She lathered her body up, holding her head downward, allowing the water to drip down her back. Just as she lifted her leg to wash in between her toes she felt Vincent's body.

"Yeah, hold that leg just like that." He growled in her ear as he entered her from behind. He pushed her against the wall of the shower and stroked her like it was going to be the last time. She couldn't help thinking of Jaheim's song 'Just in case I don't make it home tonight, let me make love to you for the last time'.

She was unaware that she had tears running down her face as her face was already wet from the shower. Twenty minutes later they emerged from the tiled shower, dripping wet, their seeds of passion washed down the drain. Vincent picked her up, carrying her naked body to the bed. He climbed atop her, licking the tears running down her face.

"You sure are sensitive these days." He whispered in her ear.

"I'm scared, Vincent. This feel so right. But I cannot handle another heartbreak. I swear that I cannot take it."

Vincent took a deep breath.

"Let's not think about heartache. Okay? Let's just enjoy each other. Obviously I'm here because I want you. That should tell you something."

Jamie nodded her head in response.

"That's my girl." He said, moving her legs apart and entering her again. "You like it when I do it to you real slow, don't you, baby?"

Chapter 21

"Mr. Henderson, you have a call on line two." Michael's secretary, Margie, high-pitched voice echoed through the intercom in his downtown loft office. It was a subsidiary of Lewar's, his grandfather's architectural firm that he'd been successfully running before Michael's father was even born. His grandfather had been looking for someone to pass the torch too. He felt confident that he'd chosen the right candidate when Michael decided to be an Architect as well.

Though, only 35, Michael was a very promising Architect. He knew before he was out of preschool that he would definitely be an artist. And, by the time that he was in the third grade he was only interested in receiving art supplies for both his birthday and Christmas. But he did his drawings more so for his own pleasure. Then he started drawing paintings for people and they would pay him. Michael never wanted for anything. He came out of his mother's womb with a silver spoon in his mouth. But he had a problem with just accepting his family's money. He wanted to make his own money. That way if he didn't want to, he wouldn't have to answer to anyone.

After winning a few art competitions in high school, Michael started to appreciate what his forefathers had created. He felt proud to follow in his grandfather and a couple of his uncle's footsteps. But it was his unique style alone that had just sealed them a 1.5 million-dollar business deal with Herschel and Timothy Pickens, two extremely wealthy brothers from the Cayman Islands. They'd researched several architectural firms and wanted their new place of business constructed using one of Lewar's blueprints as the design. They wanted no expenses spared and was willing to pay whatever was necessary to have the building of their dreams.

Michael had just taken his family's company global and was more than ready to reap the benefits. But first he had to marry his queen, Jamie. None of it would be worth it to him without her on his arm. All she had to do was stop playing hard ball and allow him to be the man. She could have whatever her heart desired, if only she was willing to let him wear the pants in their relationship.

Nobody is perfect. He thought. He felt that she shouldn't have been so quick to walk away from him when he believed he'd only showed her what a man was supposed to do for a woman.

"Take a message, Margie." Michael said, pressing the intercom button. He sat in his leather, swivel chair at his drafting table, looking at the set of pictures he held in his hand.

On one of the pictures, Jamie's naked body was laying atop her king-sized bed with some guy on top of her. She had her legs wrapped tightly around his waist, her head thrown back with a look of passion on her face.

"So, this is who is keeping her from giving her heart to me." He said in a low tone, knowing that the guy had to be none other than her baby's father. His mind drifted back to the day when Jamie first gave birth to her daughter. He'd played it real cool when she almost tripped and called him by Vincent's name. But now it was time for him to seal his place in her heart. If she didn't want him, she should have never agreed to go out with him.

No one was standing over her holding a gun up to her head when he offered to take her out to the finest restaurant in town. He had paid over two-hundred dollars on their meals alone. It had been expensive restaurants back to back up until the night that she went into labor while they were out to dinner. He wined and dined her. He kind of felt sorry for her. He knew that the buster she allowed to impregnate her probably had never taken her out on a decent date. So, no he wasn't taking no for an answer. He was going to have Jamie at all cost. And if he couldn't have her, no one else would.

"I should've ran this bum over when I saw him coming out of my woman's house." The side of Michael's face began to twitch. He could feel his anger rising. He stood, walked over to the window and looked out at the urban city.

"That ungrateful bitch got that man all around my daughter. That's my daughter. I was the one who was at the hospital when she pushed her out. I'm the first man that held her. SHE IS MINE!" He took his fist and knocked the fertility statue sitting on the table next to the window on the floor.

"I...is... everything alright, Mr. Henderson?" Margie's voice came alive over the intercom. Michael took a couple of deep breaths, wiping away the tears of rage that ran down his face. He walked over to his desk and pressed the button on the intercom.

"Everything is fine, dear. Can you come in here for a minute?"

"What can I do for you, Mr. Henderson?" Margie asked as she stood before Michael in his office.

He stared at the white middle-aged woman who was looking through her bifocal glasses. Her hair was a curly mess and she wore a long, grandma looking black dress that hid any curve that she may have had. But she was submissive. She always obeyed Michael. That was what he liked about her. As long as he worked at the firm, she was guaranteed to have a job.

"How has your son, Chase, been doing?" He asked her.

She looked at him and smiled, her overbite incredibly obvious.

"Chase is adjusting pretty well, considering."

213

"I like the sound of that." He said. "Did that donation help? I know that a school geared towards autistic students has to be kind of pricey."

"It is pricey. And, it did help. Thank you, sir."

"Now, what did I tell you about that Margie? You are to call me Michael. Sir is not necessary."

"Thank you, ugh, Michael."

No problem, Margie. You are a valuable asset to my family's firm. I appreciate all of your hard work."

Margie smiled again.

"Is there anything else I can do for you, sir? There's a potential client I'm expecting a call from."

"I love how you take your work so seriously, Margie. I wish more people were like you." Margie looked up to meet his eyes. He nodded his head and she knew what that meant.

"Yes, sir." She said as she walked over to him. She dropped to her knees, undid his belt buckle, released his penis from his pinstriped pants and took all of him in her mouth at once.

"That's it, Margie… that's it… that's it." He said as he rested his head on the back of his chair. He closed his eyes and enjoyed how she serviced him.

Twenty-five minutes later, Margie got up off her knees and reluctantly looked Michael in his face. He handed her a Kleenex and ordered her to clean him off.

"You can have the rest of the day off Margie." He said, after she was done cleaning him. "Lock up the office. I've got somewhere to be."

"Yes, sir...um- Michael." She said as she traipsed out of the room, looking down at her inward pointing toes.

Michael shut down his computer. He grabbed his work bag and stood. He put on his matching pin-striped jacket, threw his leather bag over his shoulder and walked out the office. He stopped at Margie's desk as he was heading out and handed her an envelope. "Just a little something to show my appreciation for all that you do for the firm." He smiled and winked at Margie. "Take the kid to Chuckie Cheese and maybe you could enjoy tomorrow at the spa."

"Are you saying I don't have to come in tomorrow, ugh, Michael?"

"That's exactly what I am saying, Margie. Take care, okay?" He walked out the door without saying anything else.

Chapter 22

"You did it, girl. I am so proud of you!" Jamie leaned over and hugged her best friend, Teresa. She'd just watched her, with tears of joy streaming down her face, walk across the stage to receive her bachelor's degree in Social Work.

"Thank you, Jamie. I appreciate you for staying on my case. It was hard. But I knew I could do it."

"Girl, you don't even talk the same anymore. But, I'm not complaining."

"Well, it is time I grow up, Jamie." Teresa smiled as she clutched her degree in her hand.

"I couldn't agree with you more." Jamie draped her arm around Teresa's shoulder and they walked off together.

"Ah hem." A familiar voice said. "I guess congratulations are in order."

Both Teresa and Jamie turned around to see Elaine standing there with her hand placed firmly in Jamel's hand.

Jamie took a deep breath and forced a smile. Elaine smirked.

"What's the matter, Jamie… still not used to the fact that your man married me?" A 'no-you-didn't-go-there-bitch' moan escaped from deep down within Teresa. She glared at Jamie like, "If you don't handle this, then I'm going to handle you." Jamie stepped up to Elaine, not even bothering to change her expression. She grabbed her by the face and squeezed as tightly as she could. Elaine's arms were flailing wildly. She talked a bad game. But it was obvious that she was nothing more than hot air.

"Listen to me, you little disrespectful cunt. You can have Jamel. You two are perfect together. And I cannot wait for Karma to put her foot in both of your asses. But what you will not continue to do, is to trash talk me. I've been very nice about this situation. Niceness has run out and if you say anything else to me, I am going to beat your ass for all the few cents that it is worth." She let go of Elaine. "I hope that I've made myself clear, bitch."

Teresa gave Jamie a thumbs up. She turned and glared at Elaine.

"You really need to stop. Must you rub the fact that you married Jamel in her face all of the time? You claim he is your man, right? So, leave Jamie the hell alone, okay? I've just about had it with you. I can't believe that you would bring your ole trifling behind to my graduation and try to start some mess. Either you are here to truly celebrate with me, or you can get the hell on. We are queens. And we

217

don't have time for this high school drama that you keep trying to bring. You want to keep throwing Jamel in her damn face. Don't nobody want him but you, honey. I mean, he kills bugs for a living... coming home every evening smelling like insecticides, and what not. His no-good ass is the vermin that infects rats. I don't see why you want him."

Jamel rolled his eyes at Teresa. He never liked her and now with her standing there having diarrhea at the mouth, he was reminded of why he never liked her. She talked too much for her own good. He was surprised that no man had ever stuck his foot up her behind. But she never had a man anyway, just a few juveniles that she messed around with to pass time... so that her vagina wouldn't grow cobwebs.

"Congratulations, Teresa." Jamel said to her. "I wouldn't worry about me if I were you. I'm sure ole dude you messing around with, that lil young cat that go to the junior college over there on Wilson Avenue, will be glad for you to come and play with him in his sandbox..."

"Scurry along now." He said, waving his hand at her dismissively and walking off.

"Tsk, you better run after your man, child!" Teresa said to Elaine. "He does have a tendency to fall into stray pussy!"

Jamel stuck his middle finger up, continuing to walk out the door.

"Yeah, you're real funny." Elaine said. She walked off behind Jamel. "Don't expect me to show up at your lil graduation party. I'm sure Jamie will keep you entertained."

Jamie shook her head at Elaine, thinking, *You are just pitiful*, as she walked away.

"Come on. Let's go." She said to Teresa. They walked outside into the breezy air. Teresa immediately shed her cap and gown. Just as she was about to speak, Jamie's cellular phone rang.

"Jamie, we need you here at the hospital."

"What's wrong, LaCheryl?" Jamie asked, speeding up her step. She looked around at Teresa. "I'll make this up to you, I promise."

"I'm straight." Teresa said. "You've already done enough. Go on and handle that."

"I'm on the way." Jamie said. She hung up the phone and ran to her truck. She pulled out into traffic and punched it. She was in such a hurry that she didn't have time to notice the black Hummer following her. Fifteen minutes later she pulled into the parking deck at Mercy Memorial Hospital.

"Give me the run down." She said to the charge nurse as soon as she walked onto the unit. LaCheryl followed her in her office. Jamie closed the door and put on the pair of scrubs she had tucked in her

219

bottom desk drawer. She pulled her hair back into a ponytail and was ready to assist her nurses.

"Well, first of all, Melanie just died."

"Oh, no!" Jamie said, immediately feeling her eyes swell with tears. "When did she come back?"

"Last night. She was admitted to the ICU for having Pneumonia that exacerbated her Asthma. We tried hard to save her, but she went into ARDS and there was nothing we could do."

"ARDS?" Jamie repeated, shocked. "She went into Acute Respiratory Distress Syndrome?"

"Yes." LaCheryl repeated, saddened that they couldn't save the eighteen-year-old-girl who had been so lively and determined to get better.

"Poor thing. Well, I sure hope she is at peace now." She couldn't help thinking about how she'd painted Melanie's fingernails and toenails for her the last time she was there, because it was her birthday and she was depressed because she was stuck in ICU. Jamie had even sneaked her a blue ribbon brownie from Applebee's into the Unit. She could still see the big smile plastered across her face when she pulled the brown paper sack with the brownie in it out of her work bag.

So what else is going on?" Jamie asked. She wanted to grieve Melanie's death, but she didn't have time. There were other patients who were alive she needed to help save.

"Mrs. Trowell, in bed six, has C-Difficile. That decubitus ulcer that she has on her heel is foul. It smells like somebody died in there."

Jamie shook her head, not really up for the commentary LaCheryl was giving her.

"So, what else LaCheryl?"

She looked down at her clipboard.

"Ugh, Mr. Wilkins in bed five, Cardiac output was very low. Dr. Sanchez inserted an Intra-aortic balloon pump. I'm not real familiar with a balloon pump and I don't feel comfortable taking care of him."

"Don't worry about it. I'll take care of him. You just make sure Trowell's isolation cart is fully stocked and go take care of your other patients."

"He's the only other one I have. The tech called off, so I have to go and do post-mortem care on Melanie. Her family is on the way. They want to see her before we take her down to the morgue."

"Her body is still here?" Jamie asked, feeling her eyes well with tears again.

"Yeah, she only died about an hour ago. Do you want to see her?"

"No." Jamie said adamantly.

"Are you sure? She's beautiful as ever. The only difference is that the sweet angel is not struggling to breathe anymore. She's free."

"I don't want to see her!" Jamie said, raising her voice loud enough to turn a few heads. She couldn't allow herself to get emotionally stressed, not when Mr. Wilkins had a device in his Aorta. She walked into his ICU room to assess him. He was aspirating on his own secretions.

"Let me clear that out of your lungs, baby." She said to the elderly man. She immediately picked up the yanker sitting atop his Ventilator and suctioned him. "Is that better?" She asked, leaning over him. She pulled back his covers to look at the site where the balloon had been inserted in his Aorta. Everything looked good. She walked over to the board in his room and wrote her name down as being his nurse for the day.

Just as she walked out of his room, several nurses were yelling that they were getting two gunshot victims.

"This has got to be the craziest situation I have ever heard." LaCheryl said as she walked up to Jamie to give her the details.

"So, this couple were in a domestic dispute." She said, shaking her head. "The boyfriend went and got his gun. He told the girlfriend that he would shoot her. She wrestled the gun out of his hand and it accidentally went off, shooting him instead. He got angry and snatched the gun from her. He then aimed it and shot her back. Somehow she got the gun from him again and shot him in the shoulder. They both are critical, but are expected to live. She has lost quite a bit of blood and is currently getting a blood transfusion. He, on the other hand, is irate and had to be restrained."

"You are right." Jamie mumbled. "This is crazy. So, um, what are their names?"

LaCheryl looked down at the report that the nurse in the emergency room had just called.

"Their names are Donna Kilpatrick and Marcus Donnovan."

Jamie's eyes became as wide as saucers.

"You have got to be kidding me." She said as she sunk her body down into the first available chair she saw.

The doubled doors opened. "Here they come now. Come on boss, let's get them situated."

"That bitch shot me! She fucking shot me! I'm going to kill that whore. I swear, I am." Marcus said as the nurses pulled him off the stretcher onto the hospital bed. He took a deep breath and stopped breathing. His pupils then became fixed and dilated.

Tamyra Walker

"Get the crash cart!" LaCheryl yelled.

Chapter 23

'I don't ask for much. I am a man who cares about the well-being of his family. When I decided to marry again I knew that my wife had a daughter from a previous relationship. Now how can I say I love her and not love her daughter who is a big part of her? The thing that baffles me though, is that I am the only one who seems to have love for her daughter. To say my wife hates her daughter, would be putting it nicely. Quite frankly, I am fed up'

~ Bill Marshall ~

~*~

Leanne waltzed out the front door, wearing her silk robe and her matching silk scarf on her head. In her hand she carried a cup of cappuccino and the latest edition of her Health and Wellness magazine. She sat down at the picnic table adjacent to her flower bed that held the lilies and tulips. She propped her feet up while the smell of the freshly cut lawn tickled her allergies. *Baby Come To Me* played on her IPOD. She was so engrossed in an article about the importance of mammograms that she was totally oblivious to her surroundings.

"Where's breakfast?" Bill asked, as he walked up behind her. He placed his hands on her shoulder's startling her.

"Dammit, Bill... you scared me." She said yanking her earbuds out of her ear. She clutched her heart. Her six carat wedding band sparkled in the morning sunlight that was starting to peep out from under the clouds.

Bill removed his hands from her shoulders. He sat down next to her.

"I didn't mean to startle you, Leanne." He leaned over to kiss her on the cheek. Leanne pushed his face away. "Where's breakfast?" Bill asked again, shaking off her rejection.

Leanne flipped her magazine to the next article, refusing to respond.

"I'm sure you heard me, Leanne." He was growing more and more tired of her unpleasant attitude. He knew that she knew that he hadn't done anything for her to be acting in such a jaded way towards him... nothing but told her the truth, something she didn't want to hear. Because even though it was true, sometimes the truth hurt.

"Ugh, yeah. I did hear you." Leanne finally replied. "You're capable of cooking your own breakfast, darling."

She glanced at him for a brief second.

"When you start showing me the respect that you used to show me then maybe I'll get off my pretty ass and cook for you again. Until then, you can starve for all I care. But if you're going to drop dead, can you please go somewhere else and do it? I'm trying to enjoy my coffee and magazine and don't need the distraction."

Bill walked over to his wife, grabbing her by the shoulders forcing her to look at him.

"Get your hands off me now, Bill, before I feel compelled to call the cops. You know how trigger happy they are these days. If they come here and see a burly guy such as yourself all over me... well, I'm sure you know what the outcome will be."

"Now, Leanne this has gone on long enough. Regardless of how aggravated I am with you, I get up off my butt every morning and go to work. Sometimes I don't feel like it, but I do it for our family... because the bills don't stop just because you are angry with your spouse or don't feel like it."

"Oh, this is interesting." Leanne said, referring to another article. She wanted Bill to be certain that she was ignoring him. "Oh, my God." I need to get me some of these."

"LEANNE!" Bill yelled.

"Oh, this is just amazing." Leanne said, flipping the page.

Bill stormed off in a huff. Leanne looked up and smiled evilly when she heard him cranking up his pickup truck.

Tamyra Walker

"That's right, take your ungrateful behind on down there to Wilma's lil diner. Pay that bitch to scramble you some eggs. I bet your cholesterol is elevated anyway." She lowered her eyes back to her magazine, humming along with James Ingram's crooning… "Just once, can we figure out what we've been doing wrong?"

****

Bill sat at the high bar at Wilma's diner, just a few blocks from his home, eating a nice helping of grits, eggs, link sausage, and biscuits with gravy. He took a swig of his coffee and fished his cellular phone out of his pocket. The tube television against the wall was tuned in to the *Today Show*. He smiled a little at Al Roker, standing next to Savannah, calling himself trying to cut a rug.

"How can I help you?" A voice asked.

Ugh, yeah." He said to Mr. Ogletree. "I need to come by your office today, if you are not too busy. Can you please not tell my daughter Janna about this? I…I…ugh, know she does a little work for you."

"What don't you want me to tell Janna about?" Mr. Ogletree asked. A hint of concern was mixed with his baritone voice.

"I'm divorcing, Leanne." He said without stuttering.

Mr. Ogletree let out a loud gasp.

"Come again?" he asked.

Bill held up his hand as if Mr. Ogletree could see him. "I don't want to go into detail about it right now. I'll be over to your office, say about, noonish. We can talk about it then. And, please Harold- don't try to talk me out of it. My mind is made up." He hung up the phone before Mr. Ogletree could say anything else. He took another swig from his coffee and finished his breakfast. When he was finished he wiped his mouth with the cloth napkin, dropped a ten-dollar bill on the table for the tip, and stood to leave.

As he left the register, heading for the door, Jamie walked through with Amina glued to her hip.

"Well, hello there, baby girl!" He said, embracing both Jamie and Amina at the same time.

He held her at eye level.

"Look, I am so sorry about what happened at the breakfast table that morning."

Jamie took a deep breath.

"Don't worry about it dad. I'm okay. I promise."

"No, you're not honey. Your mother was so wrong to treat you like that." He looked around the diner to make sure no one heard his conversation with his daughter. "Ugh, let me buy you breakfast,

229

honey. I know you came in here for some of Wilma's famous biscuits and preserve, right?"

"You know me so well." Jamie said with a smile. Together they walked up to the counter to place the order.

"I don't know what has gotten into me lately." Jamie admitted. "I haven't cooked a decent meal yet since I closed on my house."

"Don't beat yourself up, baby girl. You are a career oriented woman. It's okay for you not to cook sometimes, sweetie. We all know you can."

Jamie smiled again.

"You always know how to make me feel better, dad."

"Well, that's what a dad is supposed to do, honey. Now you want to tell me what's up with the poker face? I'm going to tell you what I heard the wise ole ladies back in Whitehall, Alabama saying to the young girls when I was just a kid.

"What was that?" Jamie asked.

"They use to tell them that happy girls are the prettiest. And, you are beautiful, baby, but I want you to be happy, too. So, who else has been messing with my baby? You know my rifle is always on standby."

Jamie handed Amina to her father.

"Nobody has done anything to me dad. I ugh…"

"Well… well… well." Janna said as she walked into the diner. Jamie lowered her eyes to the floor, embarrassed. She had intended to call her sister back by now. But she hadn't made the time to do so. "Looks like you're alive after all, sis." She walked over to Jamie and hugged her tightly.

"I was going to call…"

Janna put her hand up.

"Save it. I know why you were upset. I'm not saying it wasn't messed up not hearing from you… but I understand, okay. So, can we just leave it at that and enjoy breakfast together? Shoot, I'm hungry."

Tears rolled down Jamie's face. "I missed you so much." She said leaning over to hug Janna again.

"So, that means you'll agree to be my matron of honor at the wedding, right?"

"Of course I will, sis."

Bill smiled. He enjoyed the love his two daughters shared with each other.

Jamie dug into her chicken and waffles.

"I have some good news of my own, actually."

Janna and Bill both looked up from eating at the same time. Bill had decided to have him a slice of Wilma's famous apple pie, even though it was really too early in the morning for him to be eating it.

"Well?!" they said in unison.

"Well, dang!" Jamie responded with a laugh. She chewed up the perfectly seasoned chicken wings before speaking. "I want you two to meet my boyfriend."

"BOYFRIEND?! Since when did you get a boyfriend?" Janna was so excited she could hardly sit still.

"I had one all along. His name is Vincent. He is, ugh, Amina's father."

"So, I finally get to meet the mysterious guy." Janna said, spreading apple preserve on her biscuit. It's about time you stop being all secretive and what not. If I didn't know any better, I would have thought your butt was the virgin Mary."

"Don't be silly." Jamie said. She looked at Janna and rolled her eyes playfully.

Chapter 24

'I can't believe my so-called best friend let our friendship end over a man. How disloyal can anyone be? I mean, damn... what was I supposed to do? Her man was coming on to me and I truly believe that if it wasn't meant to be, we wouldn't have ended up in bed together. I did see him first. But she's always been so damn fast. She was quick to give him her phone number without knowing which one of us he truly wanted. He might've played around with her, but I am his wife. I am the Queen Bee. I refuse to let anyone break up my happy home. So, if Ms. Jamie Ferrell wants to hate me, that's her problem. To be honest, I don't like her either'

~ Elaine Franklin ~

~*~

"You can say what you want to say, Jamel, but I saw how you were gawking at her ass at the graduation. Don't try to play me for a fool."

Elaine paced the living room, with Elissa on her hip. She was crying hysterically. Her other daughter, Shanna was pulling on the tail of her shirt begging her for ice cream.

"Please, mommy, I want ice cream. Can I have some ice cream, please?"

"NO, SHANNA!" Elaine yelled, obviously taking her anger out on the little girl. "YOU'RE NOT GETTING ANY ICE CREAM. NOW GO TO YOUR ROOM BEFORE I POP YOU ON THE BEHIND." Elaine pushed Shanna towards her room. "AND DON'T COME OUT UNTIL I TELL YOU, TOO!"

Jamel shook his head at Elaine.

"You're pitiful."

Elaine ignored Jamel's comment. She walked over to the refrigerator to get a bottle for Elissa, stuck it in the microwave, and went back to yelling at Jamel.

He sat quietly on the couch, listening to her say the same thing over and over again. The yelling had been going on for a couple of weeks now. No matter what he tried to tell her to reassure her, she wasn't hearing it. She had it in her mind that he was secretly trying to get Jamie back behind her back. There was nothing no one could do or say to make her think that it was not so.

I did notice how ripe Jamie looked in that little dress she had on, hHe thought. A smile erupted across his lips as Jamie, the woman of his dreams ran across his mind.

"What are you smiling at? You're thinking about her now, aren't you?"

Jamel didn't respond. He knew that no answer was going to be the right answer and decided that it was a battle he wasn't going to choose to fight.

"I should've slapped your eyes out of your damn head. Humph. Disrespectful ass. Just going to stare at the bitch with me standing right there." Elaine slammed the door to the microwave. She sat the bottle on the counter for it to cool off.

Jamel closed his newspaper and glared at Elaine.

"Understand something, sweetheart. You can run your damn mouth until the cows come home if you want to. But the day you put your hands on me, will be the last day you put your hands on anyone."

"You don't scare me." Elaine snapped. She walked up to him and pushed him back down on the couch when he stood. "You're not going anywhere. You're going to sit here and listen to what the hell I got to say."

"Elaine, I am warning you. Please don't make me have to show you how serious I am."

"Man, whatever. Miss me with that B.S. you talking. If you keep your damn eyes to yourself and off your damn ex, we wouldn't have a problem here."

Jamel rubbed his temples.

"You are one crazy broad. I know what the hell my grandma meant now about the grass ain't always greener on the other side."

"Well, this ain't no grass we talking about. And, I don't give a damn what your grandma said. Hell, she is not my grandma. Let the ole cackling biddy say whatever she wants to say. Shit, it's a free country."

Jamel stared at her like he wanted to hit her.

"Here, take your daughter." Elaine roughly handed Elissa to Jamel. "I'm tired of her crying any way. And don't put her in the crib with a wet diaper on. Change her, please." She stormed out of the front door.

"Where are you going mommy? I want to go." Shanna said as she materialized in the doorway with her baby alive in her hand.

"Go back to your room, Shanna."

Angry tears ran down Elaine's face as she got in her Chevrolet, Equinox and drove off. She got on the interstate, driving as fast as the law would permit her without getting pulled over by a State Trooper.

Before she could stop herself she turned on Marbury Street in Glen Oaks Commons. She parked in front of the house she had shared with Eli when they were engaged. She was sure he didn't still live there. He'd only moved there because Elaine insisted that they did. She always wanted to keep up with all of her friends who made twice the amount of money that she made. They struggled hard to pay the rent and to keep the other bills paid, still, she wanted to stay there.

"I want Shanna to have the best." She said to Eli when he suggested that they rent a cheaper condo, instead of this house that was far roomier than they really needed.

"I think this is more about you than it is about Shanna, honey." Eli said. "Do we really need a four-bedroom house?"

As she sat there, wishing she could have back the life she'd had with Eli, she took a cigarette out of her glove compartment and lit it. She didn't smoke often, and she didn't do it at all around her daughters. But right now her nerves were shot. "I wish I hadn't even met Jamel." She said, tears running down her face again. "Jamie just don't know how lucky she is to not have to deal with him anymore. He is hardly at home. He rarely helps me with Elissa. Money ain't every damn thing. He needs to spend more time with her. I just know he's cheating on me. Maybe not with Jamie, but I know he's messing around. He doesn't take our vows seriously."

Tamyra Walker

An hour or so later, after she'd smoked three or four cigarettes, and somewhat calmed down, with a heavy heart, she cranked up to leave. She was about to pull off when she saw a black Nissan, Altima pull up in the drive way. "I wonder who that could be." She said as she waited to see. She half way expected it to be a real estate agent showing up to show the house to a potential buyer. Her heart sank as more memories of her and Eli's time in the house invaded her mind.

A girl who looked to be mid-twenties stepped out of the car. She stretched and rubbed her hand across her protruding belly. She had to be about five to six months pregnant. She proudly walked up to the front door of the house. But before she could get her key to unlock the door, a man came out. He smiled at her, wrapped both of his arms around her, and kissed her passionately.

"How was your day, sweetheart?" He asked.

Elaine sat there with her mouth dropped open. Even though she cheated on Eli with another man, her best friend's man, she still felt some kind of way seeing him with another woman. *So, I guess he has moved on.* She bitterly thought. *The bitches couldn't wait to get their claws in him. My scent wasn't even off him before they were ready to jump on him… thirsty behinds.*

"Oh, baby, I forgot my purse." The woman said. She turned around and walked back to the car. That's when Elaine recognized her.

It was Starletta Milner, one of her sworn enemies. She always felt that Starletta wanted her man. But she looked her straight in the face and told her that Eli wasn't her type. "Honey, you can have him. You already know that a bearded, chunky dude is not my forte." She'd said to Elaine and stormed off.

"Oh, hell, no." Elaine said stepping out of her Equinox. She was so outdone that she thought she would drop to her knees with a panic attack that very moment.

"I know damn well her lil short, no neck having ass didn't have the nerve to go behind my back and get with Eli." She ran towards Starletta as fast as she could, grabbed her by the hair, spinning her around to face her.

Starletta's eyes widened as she looked Elaine in the face.

"Yeah, it's me." Elaine said, twirling her hair up in her hand, and pulling her closer to her face. She slapped her as hard as she could with the back of her hand. "Thought you didn't want him, bitch." She spat when Starletta had gained her composure. She slapped her again. "You lying whore. I told you to stay the hell away from my man!"

Starletta held her stinging face. She was stunned as she stood there glaring at Elaine, while blood trickled from her lip that was now split.

"What have I done?" Elaine asked nervously, suddenly trembling when her rage subsided. She realized that she had assaulted a pregnant woman and could be in serious trouble. She backed away from Starletta slowly.

"How could you do this, Eli?" She asked him. She looked at him as if he had betrayed her. He had made his way over to Starletta and was comforting her.

"Do what?" He replied. "You left me for another man. I moved on with my life."

Elaine could feel her anger coming back and she wanted to lunge at Starletta again.

"I will be signing a trespassing warrant on you for assaulting my fiance." Eli yelled, as he held his deeply shaken woman in his arms.

"It's okay, Star. It's okay. She's going to jail. I promise you that she is."

Elaine dropped her head at the sight of Eli holding Starletta in his arms. With a broken heart in tow, she turned to walk away. Jamel was acting a fool and Eli didn't want her anymore. He wasn't there waiting on her like she had expected him to be. Not only had he moved on, but he had a child on the way. And he was going to make Starletta his wife. Elaine pulled off slowly. She didn't even bother to wipe away the tears that were falling down her face.

Tamyra Walker

Chapter 25

It was 12:15 on a Wednesday Afternoon. Vincent walked into *Toys R' Us* to do a little birthday shopping for his baby girl, Amina. She would be turning a year old in less than a month. And since he had taken a couple days off work, he wanted to get a head start on shopping. He and Jamie had discussed giving her a *Blue's Clues* themed birthday party. Sure it was an old cartoon, but she seemed to love it. She would sit in front of the television set for a while with her stuffed toys watching Blue. Many days, Vincent sat on the couch at Jamie's house, staring lovingly at Amina. It warmed his heart how beautiful she was, especially since she had his DNA running through her body.

"Daddy's cutie is so precious." He said aloud, as he tried to figure out what he should get that would hold her attention. The last thing that he wanted was to wait until the last minute and be unable to get what he truly felt his baby girl deserved.

'And to think I was mad at her mother when I found out she was pregnant. I feel like such an ass for that. Amina is the best thing that has ever happened to me. She brings such joy to my life. My sister loves her. My mother would love her if she took the time to get to know

her. My life wouldn't be what it is today if it wasn't for that precious little girl.

Vincent's thoughts were ripping him apart. He knew that he was wrong for how he'd acted in the beginning. He was just happy that he finally got his act together. It still hurt him how his mother treated him when he was growing up. He barely heard from her now that he was a grown man, and she lived only thirty miles away from him with a man she'd been seeing for about four years.

As far as his father was concerned, Vincent never knew the man, or any of his family. He'd asked his mother several times about his father when she was around. But she refused to tell him anything, citing that he had her in his life and that he should be grateful for that. The last thing he wanted was to take part in making an innocent child-his child, feel the way that he'd felt growing up. Especially when she didn't ask to be born.

He turned to walk on the aisle that had the Leap Frog learning toys and bumped into someone.

"I'm sorry." He said, brushing himself off. He looked up to meet the eyes of the last person he expected to see.

"Alese, is that you?" Vincent couldn't believe his eyes. Suddenly he felt the need to hide the toys he had in his hand. "I… ugh… was…"

"Just shopping for your daughter, Amina!" Alese finished his thoughts. "And, yes, Vincent. It is me." She leaned over to hug him.

"Oh, my, God, girl. You look good as ever." He said wrapping his arms around her as tight as he could. He lifted her up off the floor and she giggled childishly.

"You look good, too Vincent." Alese replied when he sat her back down on the floor.

"So, what are you doing here? Last I heard, you were in Japan."

"Yeah, I was… and I ugh, will be going back for six more months. But I am home for two weeks. Just thought I'd come and pick up a gift for my niece. You're the last person I expected to see."

"Yeah, I wasn't expecting to see you either, Alese. But I can't lie and say that I am not thrilled. I thought I would never lay eyes on you again. And here you are." He said, reaching out to touch her, "Here in the flesh."

"Yep." Alese said. She wasn't nearly as excited to see him as he was to see her. But she flashed a beautiful smile anyway and carried on like she was happy to see him. *This man ripped my heart to pieces and all I want him to do is pay.* She thought as she hid how she really felt.

"How bout we go out and grab a bite to eat?"

Alese smirked.

"I don't think that is a good idea, Vincent. From the looks of things, it appears that you are back with your baby's mother... what's her name?" She looked at the toys he held in his hand.

"Her name is Jamie."

"Whatever." Alese said, with a slight attitude.

Vincent looked at her, figuring that she had to still be hurting from how things had gone down between them. But she was standing in front of him, looking better than he remembered. He wasn't going to blow his chances, if he had any chances.

"No, baby. It's nothing like that. We share a child together, that's all."

"Humph." Alese said, picking up one of the same toys off the shelf that Vincent had in his hand. "Well, I don't know Vince. I'm not trying to hash up any old feelings."

"Vince." Vincent repeated. "See, I know you are still feeling me because Vince was your little pet name for me."

Alese smiled and looked down at her freshly painted toenails.

"It's a nice lil spot across the street that we can go to, Alese. I'm just asking to take you out to lunch. That's not too much to ask, is it?"

Tamyra Walker

Alese just stared at him. She truly felt that he had a lot of nerve to ask her to go anywhere with him after he had played her for a fool. Vincent sensed her reluctance.

"Come on now, don't make me beg... because I will." He pretended like he was going to drop to his knees.

Alese looked around, embarrassed.

"Don't make a fool out of yourself, Vincent. That definitely won't be a good look."

"So, are we going to lunch then? Since you are so worried about me making a fool out of myself."

"I guess so." Alese said, sighing heavily like she truly had something better to do. "Let me pay for this and I'll meet you over there."

"Now, that's what I like to hear." Vincent said, walking up to a separate register to pay for his items.

246

'I guess you can say that I have unfinished business concerning Vincent Hargrove. I have put it off long enough. It's time for me to handle things, once and for all'

~ Alese Middleton ~

~*~

"Dang, that was quick." Alese said as she popped the trunk to her Acura TL. She placed the packages inside, closed the trunk, and got in the car. "I knew I would see him, but I wasn't expecting it to be this soon." She cranked up the car, driving carefully across the street to Quizno's subs. *He doesn't have to know that I was discharged from the Military... that ain't none of his damn business anyway.*

As she pulled her silver, Acura TL in the first available parking spot that she saw, she was surprised to see that Vincent was already there, waiting on her. He waved at her excitedly as if he hadn't just seen her a few minutes ago. Alese smiled sadistically, applying more lipstick to her pouty lips.

"Dang girl," Vincent said, giving Alese a complete look over, when she got out of the car. "I almost forgot how incredibly beautiful you are."

Alese rolled her eyes.

"Shall we eat."

247

"Let's." Vincent said, grabbing her hand and leading the way. They ordered their food and sat down to the first available table once they had all the condiments they wanted and had fixed their drinks.

"So, how has the Air-Force been treating you? Is it as good as people portray it to be?" Vincent took a sip of his sprite.

Alese smiled.

"It is... but I am on vacation. I kind of just want to enjoy family and friends without talks of the military. I don't mean to be rude, but..."

Vincent put his hand up to stop her from going any further.

"Say no more. I was just making friendly conversation."

"So, ugh, how's your little girl, Amina doing?" Alese was eager to change the subject. She hoped that Vincent hadn't noticed how she broke out into a mild sweat when he asked her about the military.

A smile erupted across Vincent's lips. Alese felt some kind of way about the smile, but she smiled herself to play if off.

"My baby girl is perfect. She is the sweetest thing ever." He leaned forward and bit into his mesquite chicken and bacon ranch sandwich." He noticed the frown that had suddenly appeared on Alese face. But he ignored it.

"Wait." He said, a few furrows arising in his forehead. "How did you know her name? That's the second time you have said it?"

Alese shifted uncomfortably in her chair.

"It's not a problem for me to know her name is it?" She took a sip of her sweet tea, to moisten her dry mouth. "Somebody mentioned it. I forgot who."

Vincent looked at her strangely. "No, baby. It is not a problem. I was just wondering. We haven't talked. So, I knew that I wasn't the one who told you." His phone chimed, alerting him that he had a text message. He looked down at it and ignored the message.

"We don't have to talk about the Air-Force, but I am anxious to know about Japan. The culture there is totally different. How were you able to adjust?" His phone chimed again. Vincent looked down, but still chose to ignore whoever it was texting him.

"I was on a mission. My heart was broken. I didn't care how different it was. All I wanted was to…"

Vincent's phone chimed again.

"Get as far away from you as I could."

The phone chimed again.

"You might want to get that." Alese finally responded. She tried to hide the fact that she was annoyed. But it showed on her face.

Vincent looked down at the phone.

"Aww, it ain't nobody important," He said to Alese, while sending Jamie a message back. **"I'm busy right now. I'll call you in about an hour."**

"Okay." Jamie responded, inserting a kissy face emoji. Vincent turned the phone off and directed all of his attention to Alese.

"I know that I hurt you, Alese. I know that I wasn't honest about a lot of things. But if it's not too much to ask, maybe we can at least be friends."

Friends my ass, Alese thought, while taking another sip of her tea. "Sure Vince, we can be friends."

"There you go with that Vince, again." He said, smiling big.

"Give it a rest, will you? Dang, you'll run things in the ground." Alese eyes averted up to the door as she saw someone walking in. *He's fine*. She thought as she took a bite of her sandwich. She looked out the window to see what he was driving.

A hummer, huh. I don't know if that really fits him. But it is good enough for me. Her eyes followed him as he walked up to the counter to place his order. He noticed her and gave her a brief smile. She couldn't help feeling a tingling sensation that spread throughout her body, becoming more evident and lasting when it circulated like electricity down between her thighs. Instinctively she held her legs together a little tighter, shifting her hips from side to side.

"Do you know him?" Vincent asked. He noticed too that she was watching him.

Yeah, I do." She said. That wasn't exactly the truth. But it was her plan to get to know him.

The mysterious guy sat down to his table. He looked around the restaurant, his jaw becoming tight when his eyes landed on Vincent. "I know it can't be..." He mumbled as he leaned over, picking his brief case up from the floor. He pulled out a picture and glanced at it. He then looked at Vincent again.

"Oh, that's him." He said to himself, his jaw becoming tighter. "That's Vincent... the man that's been fucking my woman." He stared at him, no longer even interested in his lunch. He wanted to put a bullet in his head right then, but knew that it wasn't the right time or place. "In time motherfucker. In time." He said, focusing extra hard to calm himself down.

Vincent and Alese finished their lunch and prepared to leave. Michael's eyes followed him as he walked out of the restaurant. When Vincent wasn't paying attention, Alese turned around and winked at him. He signaled with his hand for her to call him and pointed at her car. He'd excused himself before his food was ready. He went back to his truck to get his gun, as he wasn't sure at that moment whether he was going to let Vincent live or not. Before he came back in, he left his phone number on Alese car. He knew it had to be her car. It was parked right next to Vincent's F-150. He recognized the truck now that he had recognized Vincent. She smiled and gave him a thumb's up.

You just don't know yet, sweetheart. But you're going to help me get rid of Mr. Vincent, He maliciously thought as he blew her a kiss.

"Thanks for lunch." Alese said to Vincent.

"I would kiss you." He replied. "But my breath smells like onions."

Who said I wanted your lips on me? She quietly thought, while faking a smile.

"Oh, we'll have plenty time for that... it was good seeing you, Vince."

"So, you are feeling me?" He said, sticking out his chest. "I knew it girl."

"Give me a call." She said walking off to her car.

"Umph, umph, umph." Vincent and Michael both said as she drove off.

Chapter 26

"This has been the worst day ever." Jamie said as she walked out onto the third level of the parking deck at Mercy Memorial Hospital, her place of employment for the past seven years. She popped her trunk and threw her brief case in, allowing her aggravation to show like make up on her face. She slammed the trunk close, got in the truck, and backed out of her parking space without looking back, almost backing into the Oncologist's *BMW*. Her tires screeched to a halt. She jumped out.

"I am so sorry, Dr. Owens." She said, searching his thin hairy face. He reminded her of Abraham Lincoln.

"It's okay, Nurse Ferrell. Obviously you have had a stressful day. I never see you off your P's and Q's."

"And, it'll never happen again." Jamie assured him.

"Well, good." Dr. Owens murmured, looking at his watch. "Go on home, now. You didn't hurt my car." He sped off before anything else could be said.

Jamie got back into her truck and she let the tears flow. "Lord, I try so hard to be a good nurse. I try to look out for what's in the best interest of my patients, but sometimes it's hard when you have to deal with racists patients." She said in reference to Earl Hicks, the White Supremacist she had as a patient earlier.

Two of her nurses were out sick with the flu. There was a shortage of nurses throughout the hospital. So there was no staff available to be pulled. She had no choice but to take a couple of patients so that the nurses who were there wouldn't be too overwhelmed. And to be honest, Jamie really didn't mind. She had no problem admitting that she sometimes missed strictly being a bedside nurse. Sometimes the management part of it wasn't all it was cracked up to be. The politics sometimes made her want to pull her hair out.

"I'll be your nurse today. My name is Jamie Ferrell." She said to the patient when she walked into his ICU room. He glared at her with menacing eyes. Jamie ignored his glower. She walked over to look at his ID bracelet on his arm. That was when he grabbed her by the arm and yelled, "Get your grimy nigger hands off of me.

Stunned, she took a few steps back. She took a couple breaths to get herself together.

"Sir, how are you feeling today?" She asked, trying her hardest to ignore the remark he made. He looked up at the ceiling, refusing to respond.

Fine. She thought to herself. *He doesn't have to respond if he chooses not to.* She recorded his vitals off the monitor on her clipboard, hung another bag of Rocephin on his IV pole for that nasty Urinary Tract infection that he had, and left out.

He pushed the call button an hour later, asking for medicine for chest pain. "I'll be happy to look at your chart and see what is available for you." Jamie said. She turned to walk out.

"Aye, nigger!" He said. Jamie turned around and glared at him.

"Let me tell you something." She said walking up to his bed. "You will not call me a nigger again! Do you understand me, Mr. Hicks? Now, I am your nurse and I am here to take care of you. But I don't have to take that kind of abuse from you in the process. Now like I said- I will check your chart to see what is available for you."

Mr. Hicks laughed.

"A nigger with book sense. That don't even sound right. The only thing you are qualified to do is wipe my ass, little black nigger! I remember the days when your ass would've been hanging from a tree for talking to me like that. He leaned over and spat the tobacco juice in his mouth in the emesis basin sitting on his bedside table. "Somebody need to get some order with you black people. You have gotten too far out of line."

More tears fell from Jamie's eyes as she pulled out of the parking deck. She dialed Vincent's number.

255

"Please, leave a message after the beep." It said.

Jamie took a deep breath and decided to go on and pick Amina up from Daycare even though she was getting off work early. Her bright-eyed little girl would definitely cheer her up, taking her mind off of how foul her day had been.

"You're awful early, sugar." The gray-headed owner, Mrs. Spencer, said to Jamie when she walked through the door of the daycare.

"And you look like the day has whipped you really good, child." Jamie smiled, but she didn't respond. Mrs. Spencer lifted Amina out of the playpen. "This is a little busy body here," she said handing her to her mother.

"She is that." Jamie said, smiling at her daughter. "Hey, there mama… did you miss me?" She tickled Amina's chin and she burst into a bout of giggles.

Thank you, Mrs. Spencer." Jamie said, turning to leave. She picked Amina's baby bag up and slung it across her shoulder.

"Alright, baby. You make sure you get you some rest. You could've left that child here a couple more hours. She's no problem, for real."

Jamie smiled again.

"I appreciate your concern, Mrs. Spencer. See you tomorrow." She walked out the door. She quickly strapped Amina in her car seat and got in the driver seat. Before she pulled off, she dialed Vincent's number.

"Leave a message after the beep." It said.

Jamie sighed heavily, throwing the phone in the cup holder. Amina cooed in the back as she eased her truck in drive and took off down the street.

****

Vincent looked down at his vibrating cellular phone and hit the reject button. He knew that he shouldn't have been ignoring Jamie's calls. But he was sure that nothing was wrong, and she was just calling to shoot the breeze. He would chop it up with her later. But for now, he wanted to enjoy his time with Alese. When he left her earlier, after their lunch together he couldn't stop smiling.

Before he could stop himself, he dialed her number up.

"What's up?" She answered the phone with a smile.

"Ugh, look, boo. I know we just left each other but I'm really not ready for the day to end."

"Sooooo?" Alese said.

"How bout we do dinner? Let me treat you to a real meal."

"You sure are being generous. You must think you are going to get some tonight, boy."

He laughed, "Naw, nothing like that, babe. I wasn't even thinking about that."

"Um hum, tell me anything."

"No, seriously, Alese. I just want to be in your space. That's all. I promise."

Alese was quiet. She didn't quite know how to respond to what Vincent had just said to her.

"Sooooo." Vincent spoke again. "Is it okay if I take you out to dinner?"

Alese agreed immediately.

"You just made my day, precious." He said, ending the call. He quickly showered, shaved, and dressed himself in a nice pair of jeans and polo shirt. He sprayed on some of his best smelling cologne. There was nothing that turned Alese on more than being around a man who smelled good. He wanted to impress her. Maybe then she would realize what she had in him and give him another chance.

They sat together at a little Mediterranean spot called *Taziki's*. Vincent pulled the chair out for her before he sat down himself.

"I remembered that you liked Lilies, so I got you these." He said pulling the arrangement of Lilies from behind his back.

"Oh, man." Alese said, dropping her mouth wide open. Those are so beautiful."

"They are?" Vincent asked, smiling."

"They are gorgeous, baby." She stood, walked around to Vincent's side of the table and hugged him tightly. Vincent could feel a slight bulge in his pants.

"Careful now." He said sneaking a peck on her lips. "Keep this up and I'm going to throw you across my shoulder, carry your lil fine behind to my place, lay you across my bed, and feast on you all night."

Alese nudged him playfully.

"Whatever silly!"

"Play." Vincent said as he surveyed Alese's body. She looked darn good to him and he could hardly keep his eyes, let along his hands to himself.

Chapter 27

Leanne walked down the stairs in a rush, wearing her terry cloth robe and hair rollers in her hair.

"I'm coming!" She said as she held onto the bannister, leading down to the living room.

No one ever knocked on the door that time of morning. She half way expected it to be Bill. He had been being stubborn and hadn't stayed at home in over two weeks.

"Oh, he's just pouting." Leanne had said. "Probably want me to feel bad because I wouldn't cook his old farting ass breakfast. When he gets hungry enough, he'll bring his dusty behind on home. Until then, I'm just going to enjoy the freedom, because Lord knows that man, whew, he be working my last nerve."

Leanne looked out the curtain with a smirk on her face. She just knew it was Bill standing there, looking like the lone ranger... probably was just expecting her to snap her fingers right then and some food magically appear for his hungry behind.

A slight look of disappointment colored her face when she discovered that it was not Bill after all. On the other side of the door stood a gentleman, dressed as a mail man or may be a courier.

"Hummm, I wonder who that could be!" She quickly took the deadbolt off, and smiled brightly as she remembered that she had ordered herself a few things off the QVC channel.

"Good morning." She cheerfully said, pulling her robe a little tighter around her frame.

"Good morning yourself." The mail man/courier said. He whipped out a sealed envelope and handed it to her.

Leanne narrowed her eyes into tiny slits.

"What is this?" She reached out her hand and snatched the envelope.

"You have been served." The courier said, thinking to himself, *Your mean ass is in for a surprise*. He tipped his hat, smiled, and turned on his heels, walking back down the stairs just as quickly as he had come up.

"Prick." Leanne mumbled.

She slammed the door shut and took a seat in one of the decorative armless chairs in the foyer. She opened the little drawer to the table sitting in the middle of the chairs, retrieved her letter opener, and ripped open the envelope. Suddenly her breathing became labored and her eyes quickly dried out. She opened the same drawer, grabbed her Visine eye drops, dropping a couple of drops in each eye. "Now, let me have another look at this, bullshit." She said, obviously irritated.

The Dissolution of Marriage was written in big letters on the front of the letter. Leanne immediately began to scream.

"Oh, my God. This bastard call himself divorcing me?" She threw the papers on the floor and sunk to her knees, hyperventilating, with tears running down her face.

****

Bill twilled his fingers nervously inside of his hotel room at the Mayhew Hotel on the East side of town. He sat down on the edge of the bed, flipping on the flat screen television set just to ease the loudness of the voices in his head. *Could you all have worked it out? She's been your wife for twenty years. Are you just in your feelings, and want to hurt her?*

Bill sighed with a great sense of dismay plaguing his soul. *For better or worse... till death do you part.* The voices in his head continued taunting him.

A tear rolled down his cheek. His voice trembled as he spoke. "I hate to do this, but, Lord, you know I am not happy in this farce of a marriage anymore. This has gone on long enough. I can't say anything to her without her attacking me. She takes pleasure in trying to hurt me when I gave her the very best of me. Besides, how can I lay next to a woman at night who doesn't even love her own child... a precious child she went through hours of pain to bring into the world? I've never heard of such a thing in my life." Bill rubbed his hand across the stubble on his face. "I declare, Lord. I just want some peace."

Suddenly, he felt his cellular phone vibrating in his pocket. He pulled it out, noticing that it was Leanne calling him. "She must have gotten served." He said as he hit the reject button on the phone. "I know she has because she hasn't bothered to call me in the two weeks that I have been gone... now today she wants to talk."

He took a deep breath, put on his feathered derby, that he'd gotten off his father's head when he died, and stood.

"Let me go on over here and talk to her... better now than later." He took the key which resembled a credit card out of his pocket and walked out into the dimly lit hallway. He had decided that Leanne could have the house they'd resided in for their entire marriage. He didn't need anything that big. He would settle on getting himself a two-bedroom condo somewhere downtown, close to the golfing course he often frequented. Or maybe he would move back home to White Hall. He had an inherited three-bedroom house there that he'd allowed one of his young cousins and his wife to reside in. But when his cousin got a job offer in Washington, D.C. he left the house abandoned. Bill hadn't had the time to fly to his hometown and fix it up so that he could rent it to anyone else. Honestly, he felt that house, with a little TLC, would be enough for him to live and be happy because he never intended to get married again. And if he did decide to have a relationship down the line, she would stay in her place, and he would stay in his.

Regret surged through his body like adrenaline when he turned into their driveway. Leanne met him out in the yard with a bat in her hand. This was the first time she ever came outside with rollers in her hair. She didn't have on the first shoe.

"Well, Lord, I do believe we are going to have a category eight hurricane on the Richter scale." Bill mumbled when he saw Leanne walking around on the pavement barefooted. He knew she had just gone the day before to get her toes and nails done. Today was Thursday, and she made it a habit of going to the nail shop every Wednesday regardless of whether the weather was good or bad.

She approached the car, and smashed the window on the driver's side of the car with the bat. Bill ducked to keep the shattered glass from cutting him.

"Woman, have you lost your mind?" He yelled out as a piece of the glass fell down his shirt.

"You, lowdown dirty, BASTARD!" She said, throwing the bat on the ground. How could you do this to me?" Tears streamed down her Botox injected cheeks.

"I didn't realize that you cared, Leanne. You've been so cold to me lately. I thought that you regarded me as nothing more than an irritating canker sore on the inside of your lip." He stepped out of the Cadillac Deville, pushed the little remote on his keys, to lock the door. Then he realized there was no need because his lovely wife had just broken the window.

"Now, Leanne, I'm not here to put on a scene for the world to see. If we are going to talk about this, we are going to talk like two grown and civilized adults. Do you understand?"

"Pfft!" Leanne grumbled, pacing back and forth.

"Civilized adults, Leanne." Bill repeated himself.

"Civilized, huh? That's a stretch for you, honey. You ain't been civilized since the day I met you. And were you being an adult when you had that lil motherfucker to serve me, a few hours ago?"

Bill stood, with his back against the car, watching Leanne carry on like a mad woman. He couldn't understand her logic. Just before she was served with the divorce papers, she was trying her best to teach him a lesson that he hadn't been compelled to learn. She had acted like

265

he didn't mean anything to her. Now, because he decided to no longer be her little puppet, she couldn't handle that either.

Leanne peeked over in the neighbor's yard, undoubtedly embarrassed. "Callie Frost and her husband, Will, were out in their yard when that boy brought me them papers. I know they saw everything, *Everything*, you ungrateful, pig-headed imbecile."

Bill raised his hand, "Leanne, I…"

"Nobody dumps me, Bill…NOBODY." She interrupted.

"I see." Bill said, chuckling. "So, you're not upset about the divorce. You're upset because I am the one who initiated the divorce."

"You know what, Bill. Get your ass out of my yard." Leanne lunged at him and grabbed his shirt, pulling so hard that she ripped it.

"Go on, get your weak ass back in that Deville and get the hell on. I don't need you anyway." She wiped tears and snot onto her hand. "Just know my darling. I am going to take you for everything you are worth. Do you hear me, you black bastard?"

"Leanne, you can have the house. It seems like it will do more for your self-esteem to have it. I simply want my freedom."

Anger rose up even more in Leanne. She took her foot and began kicking the car.

"Get away from here now, before I call the police on you."

Bill shook his head. He cranked up the car and left Leanne standing out in the yard acting a fool. She fell to her knees and cried some more.

"I gave him everything, all of me… and I do mean everything. And he has the nerve to divorce me. I hope the son-of-a-bitch rots in hell."

Chapter 28

"Happy birthday to you… Happy birthday to you… Happy birthday dear Amina… Happy birthday to you."

Jamie stood side by side with Vincent at their daughter's first birthday party. She was also joined by her mother, father, sister, Vincent's sister, Malina, her son Carmichael, and a few other family and friends.

Vincent held Amina in his arms while everyone gathered around her. A few minutes later, Jamie's best friend Teresa showed up.

"Sorry, I am late." She said as she walked onto Jamie's porch carrying a big bag of gifts.

"Oh, don't worry about it." Jamie said walking towards her. She leaned over and hugged her. "Thanks for coming, boo. You just don't know how much I appreciate this."

"Anything for my little cupcake." Teresa said, looking around for Amina. "Where is she?"

Jamie pointed to Vincent who still had Amina in his arms. He smiled at her like he adored her.

Teresa looked at Jamie and smiled before walking over to Vincent, reaching out her hands for Amina.

An Acura TL came up the street and slowed down a little bit as it passed by Jamie's house. Jamie noticed. She also noticed that Vincent pulled his shades down and made eye contact with whoever the person was in the car. Her hands trembled slightly as she grabbed the individual sized bags of chips to hand out to the kids.

"You, okay Jamie?" Vincent asked. Jamie didn't respond. He walked over to her and gently took the chips out of her hand.

"What you getting all worked up for?" He whispered in her ear.

"So, you notice that I am a little upset, huh?" Jamie asked, determined not to cry.

"Vincent, you have been so distant lately. Are you messing around with someone? Was that her that just passed by my house in the Acura?"

"Now is not the time for you to be acting insecure, Jamie." Vincent said with his teeth clenched. "Don't ruin our daughter's day, okay."

Jamie laughed.

"Oh, you are something else." She said, walking off when she noticed that Janna was staring at her.

"Let's cut the cake." Leanne said, walking up to the table where there were two nicely decorated Blue's clues cakes. One was a little small round one for Amina to smash. The other half sheet cake was for the guests. Leanne had made them herself. She couldn't let the day be all about her granddaughter. She was ready for people to dote on her about how good the cake was.

"That's a good idea." Jamie said, grabbing Amina and placing her in her high chair. She had on the cutest little tutu and a specially made blue's clues t-shirt that had her name on it and the number 1. The tray on the high chair was decorated in blue, white, and silver, streamers. Jamie placed the smash cake before Amina. She immediately stuck her face in it. Everyone burst into laughter as Vincent stood back, snapping pictures.

"Eat it mama." Jamie said, encouraging Amina.

****

Jamie and Janna stood together picking up all the garbage after the party was over. Vincent hadn't bothered to stick around. He'd left as soon as some of the other guests had left. He didn't even give Jamie a kiss, and that embarrassed Jamie. Her mother was gawking at them the whole time with her nose turned up. Instead of him making them appear to be a loving couple, he made it looked like he was a man who love to run the street.

Jamie's phone chimed. A smile came across her face, as she thought it was Vincent sending her a message. She sat down on the edge of one of her yard chairs and opened the text message.

Elaine: Bitch, you ain't have to invite my children to your baby's birthday party. I swear your ass is foul. Regardless of what went down between us, my babies didn't have nothing to do with it. That's alright though. I won't be inviting your funky lil behind or that lil girl of yours to my baby's birthday party either.

Jamie anticipated whether she should respond or not. Just when she was about to she received another text message.

Michael: You looked so beautiful today, wifey. I got a special gift for my sweet angel's birthday. You need to tell that chump you messing around with to keep his hands off of my baby girl. But, I'm going to handle that though, sweetie. Keep that sweet stuff wet for me, love. We'll be making love again real soon.

Jamie felt her breath being caught in her chest as she stood, looking around her. "You know what, sis?" She said to Janna. "We can finish this clean up later on." She grabbed Amina out of her high chair and carried her, as fast as she could in the house. "Come in the house. NOW, Janna!" She yelled after her sister.

Janna walked into the house, shrugging her shoulder's in confusion.

Tamyra Walker

"What in the world is going on Jamie? And please tell me the truth."

"Give me a sec." Jamie responded, dialing Vincent's number. "Please leave a message after the beep." His voice mail said in her ear.

"You know what, I don't have time for this mess." Jamie said as she ran upstairs to her room. She opened the closet and pulled all of the clothes out that Vincent had left there the few nights he'd stayed over. She threw them on the floor, running as fast as she could into the bathroom, grabbing all of his toiletries, and anything else that she saw that was his. She walked over to the pile of clothes and dropped everything else there too. She ran back downstairs, with tears streaming down her face and grabbed a big black hefty garbage bag out of the cabinet. Janna was right behind her.

"Sis, please talk to me… please. What is going on with you?"

Jamie collapsed on the staircase. She sobbed bitterly.

"It's okay, sis. I am here." Janna sat down next to her and pulled her head on her lap."

"I keep running into the same no good behind men, Janna. And I am sick of it. I'm good to all of them. And all they do is dog me like I'm just some whore in the street. Just a few weeks ago, when

Vincent's, best friend, Donna was charged with the murder of her boyfriend Marcus, I was there for him as he cried in my arms."

"Murder!" Janna repeated. "He's friends with a murderer?"

"Oh, it's such a messy story, Janna." Jamie said, lifting her head off her legs. She sat up and wiped her face. "I shouldn't be telling you this, but ugh, yeah. See, they both came in to the hospital for gunshot wounds. They'd shot each other. The only thing is, he died and she lived."

Jamie took a deep breath and stood. "She healed up quite quickly actually. And when she found out that Marcus had succumbed to his injuries she didn't seem to be the least bit remorseful. But, Vincent was upset because even though he ended his friendship with her, he still cared for her. 'She has messed her whole life up over a no good nigga.' He said to me before bursting into tears.

Jamie took a deep breath before continuing. She blew her nose, tossed the paper towel and reached for another one. Janna didn't say anything. She patiently waited for Jamie to release all of her hurt.

"Sis, I was there for him, just like I have always been. I held him in my arms. I kissed away his tears. I told him everything was going to be alright and that he could depend on me to always be there for him. But, when I had a rough day at work the other week and needed a

273

shoulder to cry on, he wasn't there. He has never damn been there for me when I needed him to."

Jamie burst into tears again.

"It's okay, sis, I am here for you. I promise I am. I will never leave your side."

"I know you are Janna, but sometimes a woman wants someone outside of family to be there... someone who she cares about. I cannot for the life of me figure out what I keep doing wrong. I know I don't deserve this."

"No, sis, you don't. I told you that you are too nice. You can't be giving your all to these crumb snatching, sorry excuse for men without knowing that they would do the same for you." She handed Jamie a Kleenex to wipe her face.

"I'm not going to lie sis... Pernell and I have had our moments. We broke up a few times because he thought I was playing with his behind about how I was going to allow him to treat me. When he saw that I wasn't going to budge, he got his act together. Our relationship is not perfect, but what we do have that makes it worth fighting for is respect for one another. Yeah, I know I am young, sis... but I think I have found my Boaz. And you can, too if you stop accepting everything that comes disguised as a man, sweetie."

Jamie took another deep breath. "You are right, Janna. You are so right. Give me a hug." They embraced for a couple minutes. Jamie loosened her grip and looked Janna in the eye.

"I have a confession, sis."

"Oh, my God. I'm listening." Janna said, half smiling.

Jamie sat back down on the staircase. She clasped her hands together. Janna leaned over, laying her head over on her shoulder. She wasn't going to rush Jamie to speak. She knew that she would when she got her bearings.

"I...I was jealous of you, sis..." She finally spoke. "Jealous of your relationship with Pernell. Part of the reason I didn't contact you was because I couldn't stand to talk to you. I was upset because it seemed as if you had all of mom's love, you had the perfect biological father, and then you had the perfect man, too. Nothing has been perfect in my life... and I know that's not your fault... but it hurts. I struggled to get through school, taking out all kinds of students loans because mom wasn't hell bent on helping me like she helped you. I went as far as I did in school because I wanted to impress her. I thought that maybe she would love me at last. But... you... Janna, momma loved you from the very beginning. She treated you like a little princess, made sure you had everything. I was broken inside... I don't understand how we could come from the same woman, and yet be so different. How could mom love you and not love me, too?"

Janna wrapped her arms around her sister and hugged her tightly. She sat up and wiped tears from her eyes.

"I'm so sorry, sis, for all you have had to go through. I don't know why momma treats you that way. You are the sweetest person ever, and the best big sister anyone could ask for."

"Didn't I tell you to stop apologizing for mom's behavior? It's not your fault."

Janna sighed. "Yeah, you did sis, but I can't help it." She leaned over and hugged Jamie again. When they let each other go, Janna looked at her and smiled weakly.

"What?" Jamie asked.

"I have a confession, too."

"I'm all ears." Jamie replied.

"I was jealous of you, too."

Jamie stood to her feet, shocked.

"Why on God's green earth would you be jealous of me?"

"I never told you, sis. But, I, ugh, I wanted to be a nurse, too. I was about to apply for nursing school and I made the mistake of asking another girl who was in nursing school how it was. She looked me square in the face and told me that it was going to be so hard. That messed me up, seriously. I was so scared sis... scared to take a chance and possibly fail."

"But her ass was in nursing school!" Jamie shouted. "If she could do it, you could have done it, too. You can't ask everybody about what you want to do, sis. Some people don't want you to have what they have. Always remember that. I swear I wish I knew who the little bitch was that told you that. Ugh, that just makes me so freaking mad. I would strangle her. I swear I would."

"Yeah, well, it's too late now. I kind of got over it after a year. And I have to admit that I am excited about being an accountant. Did I tell you that I already have a job offer?"

Jamie looked over at Janna. She pushed the stray strands of her hair out of her face and smiled.

"I am so happy for you, sis. No, I don't think you mentioned a job offer. But make sure you weigh all of your options, okay? You know I only want the best for you."

"I know sis and I am. Please believe that."

"That's good... now give me another hug, big head. I need to be planning your graduation party."

Tamyra Walker

Chapter 29

Vincent walked out his front door to meet Alese at the club. He got into his truck and immediately his mind was plagued with thoughts of Jamie. He'd dropped by the daycare to check on Amina a few times since her birthday party, but he hadn't been by the house. After a few days of non-stop calls, Jamie had finally decided to stop calling him. At first he felt relieved. He didn't want to have to lie to her about what he was up to. But he knew that if she pushed him too far he was going to break down and tell her that he was seeing his ex-fiancé again. He didn't want to have to feel guilty about what he was doing. No, Jamie didn't know about Alese, but Alese didn't know about her either. He had more history with Alese, and he felt that he should give their love another shot.

As much as he didn't want to feel guilty, he was sitting there in his driveway feeling just that way. His mind flashed back to the first night he and Jamie had made love since she'd given birth to his daughter. It had been over a year since he felt her. He desired her more than anything. She was the most passionate lover that he had ever had. He literally felt like his soul was slow dancing with her soul whenever they were intimate. It was like her love was a warm cozy blanket that he never wanted to unravel from.

He shook his head to try and ward off the thoughts. Jamie wept in his arms. She was so afraid of getting hurt again. But she allowed herself to be vulnerable. She obviously trusted him. He didn't say the words, but he made her feel as if he was going to protect her heart this time around.

Wow, I'm really an asshole. He thought as his conscience let him have it. He couldn't decide what he was going to do, if he was going to go to the club to be with Alese or if he would call Jamie up instead.

She knew what she was getting into. The blame shouldn't be all on me. Hell, she was using me from jump to get over ole boy... so why should I be sitting here feeling bad for using her, too? What's good for her is good for me.

Ten minutes later he showed up at the club. He pushed all the guilty thoughts out of his head before he entered the building, searching the crowd for Alese. He had to admit he wasn't really feeling the place. He hadn't been to the club since his daughter was born, felt as if he wasn't missing anything now. It was the same ole same ole... all the girls trying to out skank each other as far as their outfits were concerned.

"Yeah, daddy, back it up on me." A voice yelled out. Vincent turned around to find Alese in a cat suit, gyrating her butt on some random guy. Instantly, he felt himself becoming angry. He walked through the crowd, bumping a few people in the process.

The dude turned and looked him directly in the face. Vincent recognized him. It was the guy he and Alese saw at Quizno's, a few weeks back.

"I'm right here, daddy." Alese said grabbing him and pulling his head down far enough where their lips could meet without her having to stand on her toes.

DMX's *Y'all gone make me act a fool* was blasting through every speaker in the place. Vincent stood with his eyes bucked as Alese pretty much swallowed this man's face right there in front of him. He decided not to say anything after all, turned on his heels and left.

****

"Ummmmmm, that was good, boo." Michael whispered in Alese's ear. He smacked her hard on the butt. "Let's get out of here." He said, grabbing her and pulling her towards the door.

"Whatever you say." Alese mumbled, taking the olive out of her drink and popping it in her mouth. When they were outside, Michael picked her up and threw her over his shoulder. He dropped her on the passenger side in his Hummer before getting in the driver seat, taking off. Before he could unlock his front door, Alese had come out of all of her clothes. She hopped up on Michael wrapping her legs around his waist. She bit down on his bottom lip and when he parted them she shoved her tongue in as far as she could. He went from her lips, kissing her roughly, down to her perky breasts, and back to her lips again.

"Ummmmmm, yeah baby." She said as she unwrapped her legs from around his waist and stood on the floor. She still had on her heels as she walked over to his big over-sized couch. She propped herself up on the arm. "Come and get it, baby." She said, looking back at him seductively.

Michael smiled as he walked over to her with his pants dangling by his ankles. He kicked off his shoes, kicked one of his legs out of his pants. He grabbed Alese around the neck and entered her from behind before he had time to kick his other leg out of his pants.

"Oh, yeeeeeeeeeeeah, baby!" She squealed. "You got that length, baby. Work me, baby. Punish it, baby. Beat it up, baby. Have your way with it, baby!"

"Have my way with it, huh?" He whispered in her ear before he bit down on her shoulder. "You sure about that, boo?"

"Awwww, yeah, baby... It's yours baby!"

"I like the sound of that." He said as he pulled himself out of her. He turned her around, lifted her up and pushed all of himself inside of her. Her eyes rolled back in her head as she took every thrust like it was medicine to cure her evil ways. He carried her up the stairs, still thrusting in and out of her.

Throwing her down on the bed, he finally kicked his other leg out of his pants before he hopped on the bed and threw his body on top of hers. It was as if her walls were saying, "Yes master. You are the king." She wrapped her arms around his neck, in a choke hold as her legs trembled on the bed. He reached down and threw both of them over his shoulders, still thrusting in and out of her while she sang praises to his almighty soldier.

"Oh, baby, that was so good." She said afterwards as she laid in his arms.

He didn't respond. She turned over to look him in the face and his expression was dark.

She touched him on the shoulder.

"You alright, boo?"

"Shut up." He said. "I'm trying to think."

Chapter 30

Dear Jamie,

I am truly sorry for all the pain that I've caused you. I didn't realize what I had in you. I didn't know how to appreciate such a beautiful blessing. So, I messed it up. I cheated on you with your best friend. I didn't think I deserved to have someone as good as you. Instead of being thankful for you, I hurt you...

Elaine walked through the front door holding Elissa's hand. "Look who's finally walking on her own." She said. Jamel grabbed the letter he had just been writing and threw it in the desk drawer.

"That's good." He said, trying hard to disguise how fast his heart was beating.

Elaine stopped in her tracks. She glared at Jamel suspiciously.

"Honey, why are you looking so spooked? What was that you just put in the desk drawer?"

Jamel waved his hand nonchalantly. "Oh, baby, it was nothing."

"Nothing sure does have you sweating." She said running over to the desk, trying to find what he had put in there. She managed to get the letter before he could stop her. She ran in the room, closed the door and locked it to keep him from coming in.

"Open this door, Elaine." He yelled. "Open this fucking door, bitch before I kick it down."

There was no response. Nothing but silence filled the air. "Fine." Jamel yelled out. He backed up a couple of steps, took his foot and kicked the door in.

The sound of a safety on a gun being removed startled him.

"So, you think you are going to play me, huh?" Elaine was kneeling on the bed with a .38 smug nosed caliber pointed directly at Jamel's skull. Tears were running down her face.

"Whoa, shit!" Jamel said not expecting to see her with a gun.

"Put your hands up, now." Elaine ordered. She crawled off the bed, holding the gun steady. "So I give you my life, a child... and that's not enough for you, is it? Naw, you want to go running back to Jamie's ass. Is that what it is, baby? 12 hours of labor, bitch. No epidural. Enough pain to make somebody go crazy. Did you forget I had to be sewn up from the front to the back because my pussy was so mangled after I pushed out your nine-pound daughter?"

"Elaine." Jamel said, trembling. He held both of his hands up.

"Shut up, now." She said placing the gun up to his head. "Did I tell you to talk?" Tears were still running down her face. She pressed the gun hard against his head. "Is that fear I see on your face?" She asked, laughing hysterically. "I bet your ass ain't talking trash now, huh?" She said almost in a whisper as she ran the tip of the gun across his lips. "I ought to make you open your mouth and suck on this barrel bitch."

Jamel closed his eyes and silently prayed.

"Yeah, I took you from that whore. But so what? She didn't appreciate you anyway. She emasculated you, made you feel worthless. But I made you feel like a man. And. This. Is. How. You. Want. To. Repay. Me? Huh, bitch?"

Jamel didn't respond. Elaine shot a hole through the wall.

"I asked you a question, baby?" The bullet grazed the tip of his ear as it sailed past his head and lodged into the paneled wall in their bedroom.

"What do you want me to say?" Jamel asked weakly. His voice trembled with each word he said.

Elaine waved the gun in the air.

Tamyra Walker

"What I want you to do is appreciate me. I am your wife. We stood before God and the few family members that you have and said, 'I do!'"

"And, I do, baby. You got to believe me."

"Stop crying, nigga. You weren't crying just a lil while ago when you were pouring your heart out to Ms. Jamie, were you? You were ready to leave me and your baby girl behind, weren't you, you son-of-a-bitch?"

"POLICE." A loud voice echoed from the front of the house.

"What are the police doing here?" Elaine whispered, suddenly afraid.

"Here, give me the gun baby. I can hide it."

Elaine tossed the gun to Jamel and walked to the front door, sweating bullets.

She cleared her throat and put on her fakest smile.

"How are you doing today, officers? How may I help you?" She asked as she opened the front door.

"You're under arrest for trespassing and assault." The police said. "Put your hands behind your back, ma'am."

"That bitch!" Elaine yelled out as she was handcuffed and escorted out of the house.

"Don't put my mommy in jail. Please, Mr. Policeman." Shanna gently pulled on the policeman's leg.

"Get her!" The officer said to Jamel.

"Come here, sweetie." He said, unwrapping her little fingers from around the officer's pants. "Mommy is going to be okay. I'm going to go and get her. I promise."

Chapter 31

Let me get another Henny on the rocks." Vincent sat at his favorite bar, drinking his sorrows away. He couldn't believe he walked up to Alese kissing another man. His thoughts were on a rampage.

I knew there was something different about her. She just didn't seem like the same person I had fallen in love with. Maybe I hurt her too badly for her to be able to truly forgive me. I just wish she had told me that before I thought we could have another chance together.

"Well, you look like you just lost your best friend." Vincent looked next to him to see Marlena standing there, not dressed sleazy for the first time ever.

He really didn't feel like talking to her, but hearing her voice was bound to be better than hearing the voices in his head telling him how he'd screwed things up with Alese and now he'd messed around and did Jamie dirty again, too.

"What you been up to, Marlena?" Vincent asked. He turned to the side on his booth so he could look her directly in the face.

"Life's been kind of lonely without Donna, you know."

Vincent took a swig of his drink, not knowing what to say to that.

"She's in the county waiting to be sentenced. I know she's going to get at least fifteen years. The lawyer said after she shot Marcus the first time accidentally she didn't have to shoot him that second time."

"That's too bad." Vincent said, becoming angry. Truthfully he was hurt. But he was so upset with his whole life that his hurt came out sounding like anger.

"Well, that's a fucked up thing to say. Damn, Vincent. Do you have to be so cold?"

"Look..bih, ugh, Marlena, what the hell do you want? If my memory serves me correctly I believe I told you and Donna both that I didn't want anything else to do with either one of you."

Marlena took a couple of minutes to mull that insult over. Vincent sat on his stool, immediately regretting what he'd said to Marlena.

Dang, what is wrong with me? All I do is hurt people.

"I'm sorry, Marlena."

Marlena wiped a tear from her eye.

"You're good, Vincent. You have a right to be angry. Donna and I did do some pretty messed up stuff... I don't expect you to ever want to be friends with me again, but ugh, I'd like the chance to try and right some of the wrong that I did, if that is okay with you."

Vincent looked at Marlena, giving her his undivided attention.

"Shoot." He said, giving her permission to speak.

"Well, ugh, I don't know where to begin." She shook her head a couple of times. "You are probably going to hate me for this but, ugh."

"Go on." Vincent said.

"First of all, let me just say that Alese is back in town."

"Yeah, I know." Vincent said, his face suddenly becoming sad. "I saw her. We have been, ugh, seeing each other."

"I know… you might want to leave her alone Vincent. She doesn't want you for real. She never did. And I know I should have said something earlier, but she ugh, was never in the military. She was never going to marry you because, ugh…"

"Because what?" Vincent asked, standing up and staring down at Marlena as if she was his kid sister.

"Because Vincent, she was already engaged. When she supposedly came back from basic training, she was really coming back from visiting him… see he is the one who is in the Military and he had been stationed overseas in Japan."

Marlena took a deep breath.

"Don't stop now." Vincent said. "Tell me everything."

"When she came back, she was pregnant. She had her baby a couple of weeks before Jamie had hers. So, ugh, when she saw you in *Toys R' Us*, she was really getting a gift for Sarai, her daughter. Her name is Sarai Sinclair Mays.

Vincent was too outdone to say anything. Marlena continued talking. She was cheating on you all along. Even the first time when she destroyed all of your furniture for you cheating on her.

Vincent shook his head from side to side, not wanting to believe he'd been played for a fool.

"And, ugh, you know when you told us that you had gonorrhea and you didn't know if you had given it to Alese or not?"

"Yeah." Vincent responded, not knowing where she was going with that question.

"Well, Vincent, the truth is... she, ugh, see, she was the one who gave it to you. She contracted it from one of your homeboys... I... I... don't know which one."

"You mean to tell me that the bitch was fucking one of my boys and neither you nor Donna didn't say anything?"

"Well, we didn't feel it was our place. She had your nose wide open. We didn't think you would leave her, even if you did know."

She ducked, expecting Vincent to throw something. He just stood there with a blank expression on his face.

Marlena continued speaking. "Alese needed a way to break off the engagement, and when she found out about Jamie being pregnant, that was her way out. She figured that she would go and have her baby, wait till she lost all the baby weight and then come back to you… to ugh."

Vincent had his hand up to his head shaking it from side to side.

"To do what, Marlena?" He asked feeling defeated.

"To use you. She told me the other night, that while you were fawning over her like a love-crazed fool, she was going to take you for every penny you had. She was cheating on you, but she was mad at you because you got another woman pregnant. I'm so sorry that we didn't tell you. We were wrong not to tell you. We should've told you."

"Well, ain't no love lost because we're not friends anymore anyway." He said coldly. "Just tell me this though, why did you and Donna hate Jamie so much and not Alese?"

Marlena took a deep breath and stared at Vincent.

"I asked you a question." He said, trying hard not to raise his voice.

"Fine." Marlena said. "The truth is, Vincent, we knew that your relationship with Alese was not going to last. She is trifling, just like we were. But, ugh, Jamie. She was a good girl. We knew that she loved you. We could see it. But we didn't want to lose you. I had no idea that Donna had done what she did to you. But I wanted you for myself, too. When Jamie came along she made us feel low. She was so successful and we were nothing but lil hood rats. She was beautiful and so smart, and just everything that we weren't."

"I've heard enough." Vincent yelled. "Just so you know- you disgust me, Marlena. And I hope that I never see your ratchet face again." He threw money on the counter to pay for his drinks and stormed out of the bar, refusing to look back.

Marlena ran out of the bar behind him.

"Wait, Vincent!" She yelled. "She's seeing some other guy now named Michael."

"Yeah I'm assuming that must be the guy whose tongue was all down her throat the other day." He didn't slow up his pace.

"Well, his name is Michael and he drives a black Hummer."

"A what?" Vincent asked as he stopped in his tracks.

"A black hummer." Marlena repeated. "What's the matter?"

293

"What else do you know about him Marlena? Do you know his address? Anything?

"No, I'm sorry. I just know that he is rich that's all."

Vincent turned on his heels, running as fast as he could. He picked up his phone dialing Jamie's number, but she sent him straight to voicemail.

"Dammit, baby girl. I'm so sorry, boo!" he said as he hopped in his truck and put his foot on the accelerator.

Chapter 32

So, where are we going, boo?" Alese asked Michael. She linked her arm through his, snuggling up close to him.

"How about dinner, baby?"

"Sounds good to me." She said. "Let me just call mom and make sure she doesn't mind watching Sarai for me." She picked up her phone. The battery said two percent.

"Aww, man." She whined. "I need to use your phone, sweetheart. Mine is about to power down."

"Sure thing." Michael said, putting in the code for her and handing her the phone. Alese dialed her mother's number.

"Mom." She said when she picked up the phone. "Do you mind watching Sarai for me for a few hours? I'm out on business... yeah... no, mom I'm out of town."

Michael shook his head at how Alese was sitting there lying to her mother. "Lying ass thot." He said in his head.

"I should be back in town in a few hours. Just make sure she eats. She has food in her bag, and give her a kiss for me, will you? Okay mom, love you... bye." Alese hung up the phone. Michael had his attention fully on the road so she decided to snoop through his phone. She went straight to his text messages. There was this one particular number that he constantly sent messages to. It was under the name, "My wifey."

"Wifey." Alese said to herself, feeling a tinge of jealousy. She peered over at Michael to make sure that he wasn't paying her any attention. When she knew that the coast was clear, she hit send on the number. As the phone rang, she was surprised at the picture that she saw on the screen.

BAP... BAP... BAP! She felt several slaps across her face. Her head hit the side of the window on the passenger side. "Who told you to go through my phone?" An angry Michael asked her.

"So, you fucking this bitch, too?" Alese asked turning the phone towards him so he could see the picture. "I swear I'm sick of this whore."

He punched her in the nose. Blood immediately began to spew out.

"Don't you ever fix your mouth to call my wife a bitch and a whore." He spat.

"You know what? Let me out of this mother..."

"BAP... BAP... BAP! He slapped her a few more times. "Shut up, now. You're not going anywhere. You was flirting with me all in front of that bitch you was with. You wanted to fuck me. And now, you think you're going to leave? Sit your lil narrow behind back and shut up, now." Alese cut her eyes at him. He took out his switch blade. "Cut your eyes at me one more time... just one more time." Michael yelled.

****

Jamel dropped Shanna and Elissa off over to their grandmother's house. "Daddy will see y'all in a few hours." He said as he gave both of the girls a kiss. He watched until his wife's mother, Daisy, disappeared behind the door before he drove off.

It took him twenty-five minutes to get to the jail to pick Elaine up. He couldn't bail her out. It was mandatory that she went before the judge. Now that she had gone before the judge he was sitting, patiently waiting for her to be released from jail.

"I missed you so much." He said to her, kissing her on the forehead when she walked out and got in the truck.

"I missed you too, babe." She said. "But I am so hungry. Can we please go and get something to eat?"

Jamel laughed. "Sure thing, baby! What do you want."

"It don't even matter, boo. Just get me something and quick."

"Well, let's hit that new Golden Corral up over there on Swanson Blvd."

"Let's do it." Elaine said, strapping on her seatbelt and turning the radio up. "Aye, that's my jam!" She said in reference to Fantasia's song, *Two Weeks-Notice.*

Jamel smiled and focused his attention on the road.

****

Alese sat in the truck with Michael crying her eyes out. He'd beaten her black and blue and still was hitting her every time he thought about how angry he was that she'd snooped through his phone. Then, to make matters worse, she had called Jamie a bitch. That was a big no-no. No one was allowed to say anything foul about his woman.... his soon to be wife. So he thought.

"Wipe them damn tears from your eyes. You weren't crying when you were popping off at the mouth, were you? I bet you wish you hadn't never met me now, don't you?"

He laughed. "I swear you look ridiculous. All you women are the same... think y'all run shit. You don't run nothing. I took you from that ole no good, thug looking... speak of the devil- there go that punk now."

Alese quickly unsnapped her seatbelt, opened the door and jumped out.

"Fuck her." Michael said as he put his foot on the gas and sped up. "It's about time I put this son-of-a-bitch out of his misery." He said, rocking back and forth with a big smile plastered across his face.

****

"There that fool goes now, driving like a bat out of hell." Vincent looked up in his rearview mirror and saw Michael driving really fast behind him.

"What does he think he's doing?" He said as he switched lanes before he could hit the back of his truck. He dialed 911 on his phone and quickly pulled over to the nearest gas station.

"That punk scared." Michael said, laughing hysterically. "Look at him. I don't know what the hell Jamie ever saw in him."

"Oh, all my jams are playing today!" Elaine said with a grin on her face. "I don't know when the last time I heard a song by SWV… WATCH OUT BABY!"

BOOM. Michael crashed his hummer into the side of Jamel and Elaine's Chevrolet Equinox. The truck then began spinning around before it smashed into a pole. Michael was immediately ejected. Elaine went through the windshield of the Equinox.

Chapter 33

"I am going to miss you guys." Jamie sat in the break room with her staff. It was her last day as the unit manager and they were having her a farewell party.

"We are going to miss you, too." LaCheryl replied. "I hope I make as good of a unit manager as you did."

"Oh, you will do just fine, LaCheryl. What I told you about doubting yourself? You have been a nurse longer than I have and, girl- you know your stuff."

"Thanks to you." LaCheryl stood and walked around the table to hug Jamie. "You brought such joy to this unit. Things are not going to be the same without you."

"Awwwww." Jamie said, wiping tears of joy from her eyes. "I'm dying for a piece of this cake. Somebody grab me a knife so I can cut it, please."

"JAMIE, LACHERYL... I NEED YOU TWO TO COME OUT ON THE UNIT NOW."

"What's wrong?" Jamie asked, immediately standing.

"There's been a horrible accident. E.R. is running a code on one of the victims now."

"I'll go down there and help them." LaCheryl said as she grabbed her stethoscope and ran.

"Okay, let's get a couple of rooms prepped. I don't know how bad it's going to be. But let's try and be ready." Jamie said, feeling a surge of adrenaline coursing her veins.

Two hours later…

"LaCheryl where are you? We are about to get the first patient from E.R." LaCheryl sat in Jamie's office with her legs up in her chest. She was trembling like she had just finished watching a horror movie. Tears ran down both of her cheeks.

"What's wrong with you?" Jamie asked walking up to her. She kneeled down next to LaCheryl, handing her a Kleenex. "Here, girl. Wipe your face and tell me what's up."

"That man was EVIL… he was pure evil."

Jamie took a deep breath.

"LaCheryl, hun, are you alright? Who was evil? What are you talking about?"

"That man. The one I helped run the code on. It was like he had nine lives. We revived him several times, and every time we got him back, he sat up and said, "My feet are burning. It was like his ass was in Hell's fire before he even expired."

"So, he didn't make it?"

"No, he didn't make it… but he's in ICU four and I can't bear to look at him." LaCheryl burst into tears. "I will quit this damn job today if I have to go in that room with that, man."

"Calm, down, LaCheryl. Now it can't be that bad. If it is that bothersome to you, I will go in there and do post mortem care on him."

"Would you?"

"Sure, LaCheryl. But you need to pull yourself together…"

"Code blue, ICU NINE, Code blue ICU NINE, Code blue ICU NINE." Magda, a nurse off 3 West who had been pulled to the unit, was standing at the nurse's station calling the code."

Jamie ran to ICU 9. "What do we have here?" She asked, stopping dead in her tracks when she saw that the patient lying lifeless on the bed was her ex best friend Elaine.

"What are you waiting on, Jamie?!" LaCheryl yelled. "Get in here and do chest compressions."

Jamie stared at Elaine. She didn't know at that moment if what she felt was sympathy or contempt. *What's the matter, Jamie… still can't handle the fact that your man married me?* Every foul thing that

Elaine had said to her in the past year ran through her mind. The bitch had done her very best to break her, and now she was lying there, hurt, needing Jamie to help save her.

Let the bitch die… no that wouldn't be right. You are a nurse… naw, fuck that. That whore tried to hurt you with everything in her… save her Jamie… let her die!

Slowly, Jamie got her feet to transition the way she needed them to. She walked over to the bed. She put her trembling hands in the middle of Elaine's chest and began to count the compressions.

"One… two… three… four… five… six…" *No, I'm not going to let you die. It is my job to save people. I'm not responsible for how you treated me. But right now, I'm going to put all of me into saving you. Death is too easy for you.*

After two rounds of Epi, Elaine once again had a steady heartbeat. Jamie looked at her one last time, took off her gloves, and slowly walked out of the ICU. When she heard Jamel's voice yelling from ICU ten, she already knew it was him. He was critical but was conscious. She chose not to go to his room. There were already two other nurses in his room.

"This has been some day." She mumbled as she walked to her office, closed the door and cried. She was ashamed that she'd even thought for one second that Elaine deserved to die. "Lord, please forgive me. I was wrong. Please forgive me, Lord."

When she was done asking God for forgiveness, she wiped her face and nose. "I promised LaCheryl I would get that deceased patient ready for her." She walked out of her office and approached ICU, room number four. She pulled the curtain back, walking over to the deceased. She yanked the covers back that covered his face and immediately began to throw up. Michael Henderson, the man who'd terrorized her for over a year was lying on the bed. His eyes were wide open and they were affixed on her.

"Oh, my God... I can't do this... I can't do this..." She ran to the door, turning around at the door. "I can do this... I am a nurse. Yes, I can do this." Slowly, she walked back over to the bed. His eyes were still staring at her. She reached for his arm to take the IV out. He reached up and grabbed her hand, as he still had a few reflexes.

"SOMEBODY HELP ME!" She yelled out. Every nurse in the unit came running to her rescue. "He grabbed me. Oh, my, God he grabbed me." She was hysterical. Madga grabbed her. "It's okay, hun. It probably was just his reflexes. Somebody get her out of here." She said, taking control over the situation.

Magda stuck her head out from behind the curtain. "Jamie. Please notify the deceased's spouse that he expired."

"SPOUSE?!" Jamie yelled out. "YOU MEAN TO TELL ME HE WAS MARRIED?"

Epilogue

Jamie was filled with regret as she prepared herself to do the unthinkable. "How can I ever look that man's wife in the face, when I was having her husband. I swear, God, I didn't know that he was married. I may be a lot of things. But I would never take part in adultery."

Jamie sat atop her desk, with tears once more streaming down her face. Her last day as Unit manager had turned out to be one of the worst days of her life. She was mentally exhausted and just wanted to go home to her daughter.

She dragged her feet to the waiting room, that was right outside of the ICU. Poking her head in the door she said, "Ugh, I am looking for Julia Henderson. Is she here in the waiting room?" Everyone looked around to see who Julia could possibly be. No Julia came forth.

Jamie sighed heavily. "Maybe she went to get a cup of coffee. I'll check and see if she went to the vending machine."

A guy wearing skinny jeans and a buttoned down shirt spoke up. "Is this about Michael Henderson?"

Jamie turned on her heels. "Ah, yes it is. Are you related to him?" She looked at his face really hard. He was the same complexion as

Michael. *Well, what do you know, he didn't even tell me he had a brother.*

The guy stood, and pulled off his hat revealing his long curly hair. It was a reddish looking color at the end. He looked familiar to Jamie. She could have sworn she knew him from somewhere.

"I guess you could say that." He said. "I don't know who the hell Julia Henderson is. But I am Julian Henderson, and Michael is my husband."

"Your what?" Jamie asked, totally shocked.

"He's my husband, sweetheart. Now, how is he? Any updates?" Julian crossed his arms across his chest, batting his eyes at Jamie. He had more mascara on his lashes than she had on hers.

Jamie just stood there with her heart beating fast.

"He's, ugh, he's… he's…"

"He's what, honey?" Julian asked, snapping his fingers. "Is the son-of-a-bitch dead?"

"Ah, yes!"

A long tear slid down Julian's face.

"That serves that cheating bastard right. That's what he gets for running around on me with…"

Julian finally looked up at Jamie. His mouth dropped wide open.

"It was you... **you**." He said pointing at her. Everyone began to stare at her and whisper under their breaths. A few of them were laughing. "You... you were the one who was sleeping with my husband in my bed."

Jamie was speechless. Her mouth kept opening but no words would come out.

"What's the matter, nurse... cat got your tongue?" See, I knew the hussy was cheating on me. So, I installed a nanny cam. And yes, honey that was you in my bed. I have to say that your face is just as pretty as your ass, hun."

Jamie began to hyperventilate.

"Lord, this can't be happening. This is too much, Lord. Lord, please deliver me from this situation. Please. Lord. Right. Now. Lord."

Julian clapped his hands.

"Bravo, honey bun. So, now you want God? Well ain't that some shit? You didn't want God when you were riding my husband to kingdom come. I know it wasn't Shirley Caesar serenading you two disrespectful hoochie mama's when you were making love faces in my damn bed. My bed, bitch." He grabbed his helmet lying next to him and walked towards the door. "Well, nurse, thank you for your time.

You can send that cheating bastard on to Greene's funeral home.... but I just want you to know," He took his shades off so he could look Jamie directly in the face. "You'll be seeing me, missy!"

The End